MW00986120

ELIZA

Shawn Winchell

This book is a work of fiction. The names, characters, and events portrayed in it are the product of the author's imagination. Any resemblance to actual persons, living or dead, events, or localities is entirely coincidental.

Copyright © 2021 by Shawn Winchell

All rights reserved. No part of this publication may be reproduced, stored or transmitted in any form or by any means, electronic, mechanical, photocopying, recording, scanning, or otherwise without written permission from the publisher. It is illegal to copy this book, post it to a website, or distribute it by any other means without permission.

ISBN: 9798525392861 (paperback)

www.shawnwinchell.com

ELIZA

Shawn Winchell

60 YEARS AGO

The sky was the deep royal blue of just after dusk. There were no streetlights on the two-lane highway. No stars, no moon, no traffic. Just the barrage of the evening air trying to get in through the open window of the truck against the music trying to get out of it. Something bounced across the beam of the headlights. The man assumed it was some kind of animal.

"What was that?" the woman in the passenger seat asked.

"Don't matter," said the man, looking at her. "It's gone."

When he turned his eyes back to the road, a young girl ran into his lane. She faced the truck and froze—her wide eyes glowing in the headlights. He stomped both feet onto the brake pedal. The woman's head slammed into the dashboard as the truck squealed to a stop. The man clicked off the radio and turned to the woman.

“You all right?”

“I’ll live,” she said, rubbing her forehead. She gestured out the windshield. “Will she?”

The man put the truck in neutral, set the parking brake, and opened the door. He moved toward the front of the truck, refusing to look at anything except the bumper, afraid of what he was sure would be lying in the road. A few dead bugs were splattered on the chrome but nothing else. Slowly, he turned his gaze toward the pavement. More nothing. It did not make any sense. If he had not hit the girl, then where did she go?

“Hello? Is someone out here?”

The man continued looking around. He saw just his truck and the deserted highway. No body. Nobody. He walked to the shoulder thinking the girl must have run off. All he could see were the silhouettes of the trees. Shaking his head, he turned back toward the cab of the truck. His foot hit something. He looked down. A red tennis ball. He bent down to pick it up. As he did, a slight breeze blew across his face and he thought he could hear a child laughing.

1

Mason Turlock smiled as he turned off of Highway 63, away from the sunset. Northwestern Hospital for the Mentally Unstable—known around town as the Farm—was just a mile up the road. Amber had been talking about visiting it forever. She was way too into all of that haunted, ghost-hunter crap as far as Mason was concerned but he wanted to make sure she was in the best possible mood before he gave her the news. He had quit his job for the third time that year.

Amber sat blindfolded in the passenger seat. Their Australian shepherd, Jacoby, asleep in the back. It had taken quite a lot of convincing to get her to go along with a surprise date, especially since she hated letting anyone else drive her car. Mason had not had a car of his own since they graduated high school. He traded in his '91 Corolla for a 2002 Honda Valkyrie. He'd ridden that bike ever since.

The Farm was a series of buildings at the center of a large plot of farmland. Or... it used to be. The asylum had been abandoned fifty-eight years ago. Now it was nothing more than several acres of weeds and dry soil surrounding a cluster of decaying buildings. All that remained of the main building was a moss-covered mass of cracked and faded tiles on top of three rotting walls. The fourth might have been ripped away by the weather or broken down by years of neglect. Either way, the remains of the missing wall were littered throughout the cracked dirt surrounding the building.

As Mason slowed the car to a stop, Jacoby whimpered.

"You're okay, buddy," Mason said to him. He put the car in park and cracked open a window. "Don't take that off yet," he said to Amber.

Mason got out and ran around the car to open the door for her. He led her by the arm into the abandoned asylum.

Despite the balmy late-September air, it was cold inside the building. Streaks of sunlight stretched across the floor through numerous holes and cracks in the walls. Dead vines crunched beneath their feet with each step. Mason took a blanket out of his bag and laid it out on the floor. He lit the three-wick candle that he had brought, not to set the romantic mood he had hoped, but to cover the stale, musty scent of decay and what he hoped was animal piss.

"Okay," he said, "you can take off the blindfold."

***

Mason met Amber on the first day of fourth grade. Her family had just moved to town and she did not know anyone when she started school. Mason took it upon himself to welcome her to Mrs. Branson's class. He kicked her chair out as she was trying to sit down.

The entire class broke out in laughter. Her knee scraped against the desk as she fell and she began to cry.

"Mason!" Mrs. Branson yelled. "You need to apologize to Amber right this second. And after you have helped her up, you can escort her to the nurse on your way to the principal's office."

Mason did not look at Amber as he reached out to help her up. Mrs. Branson just did not understand good humor.

Amber glared at him as she took his hand and climbed to her feet.

"Thanks," she hissed.

They made their way out of the classroom.

"That wasn't very nice, you know," Amber said once they were in the empty hallway.

"Oh come on," Mason said, "it was funny. Everyone else thought so."

"Not me. I could have really gotten hurt."

"Well... did you?"

"No. I guess not."

"See? So it was funny."

"Okay, fine. Whatever."

"But if you *had* gotten hurt, then it would have been hilarious." Mason said, laughing at his own joke.

Amber glared at him again and decided it was not worth trying to talk to such an immature boy. She switched to the silent treatment, which lasted for about as long as it took them to pass four closed classroom doors and turn the corner.

"You know," she said, "you are the first person I have talked to since we moved here. Well... other than the ghost in my dining room. But you are the first living person I've talked to."

"Ghosts aren't real," Mason said.

"Yes they are! He lives in my dining room. I think our house used to be his before he died. He won't tell me though. He doesn't really talk. He just watches us. Whenever I try to talk to him, he starts shaking and disappears. I think he is shy."

"He's probably just getting ready to possess you."

"Shut up," Amber said, but she was smiling.

Mason threw his arms out to the side and waved them around.

"Ooooo... Amber..." he said in his best ghost voice, "I'm going to take over your body."

They both laughed the rest of the way to the nurse's office.

***

Amber tucked her chin as she untied the handkerchief that had been wrapped around her eyes. Dead weeds ran along the floor and up the cracked walls. As she raised her head, she saw a pile of rotted drywall that used to be the counter where new patients checked into the asylum. Behind it, a metal sign hung down from the ceiling. The letters and numbers on the sign were buried beneath decades of dust, but enough was still visible to see that it used to be a directory. A rusty gurney and a wooden wheelchair with a broken wheel sat next to the mouth of a wide hallway. Light fixtures dangled from the ceiling every four feet. Some still had the jagged bases of broken light bulbs screwed into them, but most were empty. Stolen, most likely. Amber blinked away the darkness and her eyes adjusted to the candlelight. She smiled and shoved Mason's shoulder with both hands.

"I thought you didn't believe in any of this stuff?"

"I don't," Mason said, smirking. Amber loved that smirk. She called it his used-car smile. All he had to do was flash it and he could sell anything to anyone. She always told him it was a mistake when he quit that job.

Mason had started and quit seven different jobs in the two years since he left the car lot. And he always gave the same excuse when he quit another job. *He just wasn't feeling it.* Amber supposed that meant he could not see himself doing it every day for thirty or forty years, which she could understand. But he never even gave any of those jobs a real chance, and they had bills to pay. At some point, he was going to have to suck it up and pick one. How else would they ever be able to start a family?

"Wait here," Mason said. "I'll go get Jacoby before we take the grand tour."

The car was rocking back and forth on its axles when Mason approached it, like something from an old *Steamboat Willie* cartoon. As he got closer to the car, he heard Jacoby yelping. Once he was close enough that the glare of the sunset was no longer blocking his view into the windows, Mason could see Jacoby throwing himself from side to side in between yelps—like he was trying to break the windows. When Mason opened the door, Jacoby cowered away from him and the yelps became whimpers.

"Come on, boy," Mason said. He clipped a leash to Jacoby's collar but the dog refused to leave the car. Mason grabbed him around the hips and pulled. The dog's back arched and all four legs stiffened as he dug his claws into the seat.

"Jacoby," Mason snapped and kept pulling. "Let... go... we are going... for a... walk."

Jacoby kept his claws firmly dug into the leather.

"You are not going to ruin this for me," Mason said as he climbed into the backseat. He wrapped Jacoby up in his arms and pushed against the closed door with his foot. Still Jacoby held on. Mason repositioned himself so that he could get both feet up on the door and kicked off as hard as he could. The two of them tumbled out of the car onto the ground. Mason landed on his back and lost his grip around the dog's waist. Jacoby bounced to his feet and took off running, barking as loud as he could as he went.

Amber heard the barking and came out of the building. She saw Mason lying on his back by the car.

"Are you—" She was cut off by Jacoby sprinting past her. "Mason, hurry! We have to catch him."

Amber did not wait for a response before running after their dog. Mason groaned as he rolled over and pushed himself to his feet. He followed Amber but only at a light jog. That stupid dog would come back eventually. He always did. But if he didn't this time, it would be Mason's fault. *Who else could be blamed? It had been his idea to bring Jacoby along. Amber hadn't even known where they were going.* At that thought, Mason started running a little faster and calling for

Jacoby. Not that it would matter. Mason had taken that dog through three rounds of obedience training and he still never listened.

Mason saw Amber standing on top of a small hill. He slowed down to his original pace. As he got closer, he saw her hands covering her gaping mouth. Her eyes were wider than he had ever seen them. He reached the top of the hill and put a hand on her shoulder, about to ask if she was all right. Then he saw Jacoby.

The Farm had an on-site graveyard. It was used for the patients that experienced one particular negative side effect that was an inherent risk of their treatment. From the look of it, this was a common side effect. Jacoby was in-between three headstones, hopping and twisting in the air, alternating between growling, crying, and barking.

Mason, still with one hand on Amber's shoulder, squeezed her hands with his other. He pulled her hands away from her mouth and wiped a tear off of her cheek.

"I'll get him," he said.

The closer Mason got to Jacoby, the more violently the dog thrashed. The noises coming from the six-year-old Australian shepherd grew louder with each step that Mason took. He held his hand out—palm down—and spoke quietly as he moved closer to his dog.

"Jacoby... you're okay... it's me, buddy... it's all right..." Jacoby either could not hear him or did not care to listen. The dog continued his trance-like flailing.

Mason decided to try a different approach. He bent his knees and crouched down, now only a few feet away from Jacoby. With his hands hanging at waist-level and his arms bent at forty five degree angles, he took one more step and loaded his weight onto his front leg.

"Sorry buddy," he said under his breath as he sprung forward and tackled his dog. He timed it so that he was able to wrap his arms around Jacoby's stomach just as the dog's feet left the ground. Jacoby let out a high pitched cry as Mason made contact.

Amber gasped.

Jacoby's lips pulled back and his jaw clenched, showing off his well-maintained but slightly yellow teeth. His nose twitched as he growled while continuing to whip his head around.

Mason somehow managed to maintain his grip around Jacoby. He squeezed just tight enough on Jacoby's ribs so that they were not able to expand when the dog took a breath. Mason tried to soothe Jacoby with his voice. Jacoby kept snarling.

"A little help," Mason called to Amber.

She rushed over to them, then hesitated before reaching out to the dog. After trying to pet him a few times, but flinching each time he thrashed his head, she placed her hand between his ears and held it there. Slowly, she began to rotate her wrist and shushed him the way that she imagined she would a baby if Mason ever got on board with the idea of having kids.

Jacoby looked up at her and his lips began to relax. He let out one last growl, then started panting excitedly enjoying the extra attention he was getting from Mason and Amber.

"I told you this place was haunted."

"Whatever you say," Mason said.

"How else would you explain what just happened? You know animals are more sensitive to ghosts than we are."

"What I *know* is that Jacoby hates being left in the car." Mason gave their dog a couple of hearty pats on the side and got up off of the ground. He wiped the dirt from his hands and forearms onto his jeans. "I'm starving. Let's save the tour for after we eat."

Mason handed the leash to Amber and finished brushing himself off as she went back toward the main building. He clapped his hands a couple of times to get the last of the dirt off of them. He took a step to start after Amber but his foot hit something. A red tennis ball. He had not noticed it before. Then again, he had been a little preoccupied. Mason bent down and picked up the ball. He looked around but all he could see was Amber heading down the hill with Jacoby, a handful of trees with leaves that were just beginning to change color, and a bunch of tombstones. He shrugged. Mason threw the ball across the graveyard toward the trees and took off after Amber and Jacoby.

When they sat down in the candlelit asylum for the strangest romantic meal Mason had ever heard of, he forgot all about his ulterior motive for the date and simply enjoyed debating the merits of various paranormal phenomena—including what they had just witnessed with Jacoby—with Amber. The dog was seemingly unaware that anything out of the ordinary had happened and was himself simply enjoying the bowl of water that Amber had set out for him while not-so-stealthily stealing bites of food off of Mason's plate.

As the sunset coming through the cracked walls gave way to starlight, Mason opened a second bottle of wine and poured them both another glass.

"What about reincarnation?" Amber asked. "Haven't you heard about those kids who somehow know every little detail about some person they've never even heard of? How do you explain that?"

"Easy. It's the parents. They do it for the publicity. Or they fell asleep with the TV on some biopic that the kid ends up watching."

Mason did not hear Amber's response. He got distracted when something hit the back of his hip. He turned to see what it was, bracing himself for the possibility of it being something like a rat. It wasn't a rodent. Sitting behind him, just off the blanket, was a red tennis ball.

Amber was still giving her rebuttal, but it was just white noise to Mason. He looked around the room. It was dark, but he could tell that they were the only ones there. He grabbed the ball and tossed it toward the dark hallway. He finished off his glass of wine with a single gulp.

"More?" He raised the bottle in Amber's direction. She shrugged and nodded as he topped off her glass before emptying the rest of the bottle into his own. Amber continued to educate him on the validity of past-life experiences. She was never going to change his mind though. Mason could barely hear what she was saying anyway. He was focused on the sound of the ball echoing down the hallway away from them.

Jacoby, who had been sleeping since finishing off Mason's meal, bolted upright. He began to growl. Mason downed his glass of wine again and looked back at the hallway. The red tennis ball bounced out of the darkness of the hallway into the flickering orange light of the candle.

"Uh-huh. Makes sense," Mason said over the top of whatever it was that Amber was trying to convince him of. The ball continued to bounce toward him. "Let's get out of here."

"Oh... okay sure." She took a sip of her wine and wrapped her arms around him. "Thank you for this. Tonight was so much fun," she whispered into his ear.

"That's great," Mason said, glancing over his shoulder. The ball was getting closer. "Glad you had a good time."

Mason helped Amber stand up off of the floor. He grabbed the bag that he brought their dinner in and Jacoby's leash but left the blanket, candle, and empty wine bottles on the floor. He nudged Amber toward the door with the bag.

"What about the rest of our stuff?"

"We have enough blankets," Mason said as he bent down and blew out the candle.

2

"Mason? Come on back." The receptionist was new. Or, at least new enough that she did not know who he was.

When he had pulled into the parking lot, Jeremy had been right there to greet him. Just like Mason had taught him.

"Looking to finally trade in that old bike?" Jeremy asked.

"No way," Mason said. "Got a meeting with the boss."

"Great!" Jeremy flashed a smile at Mason, showing off his professionally whitened teeth. That was a nice touch—much better than the nicotine and coffee stains that Mason remembered. "You remember where the office is at. Good luck. God knows we could use the fresh blood." He winked at Mason and walked deeper into the car lot to find his next target.

Mason stood up from his chair in the lobby. The receptionist led him past the counter full of complimentary drinks for customers to a closed door. She knocked once and opened it.

"Mr. White, I have Mason..." she paused to look down at her clipboard, "Turlock here for you."

Mason gave her a nod as he squeezed past her into the office. A robust man stood up from behind the desk and took Mason's hand with both of his.

"Mason. Good to see you. How've you been?"

"Mr. White," Mason said, trying to get his hand free from the over-enthusiastic shake.

"None of that, Mason." He pulled Mason's hand back and kept shaking. "Uncle Jim. Please. You know that *Mr. White* business makes me feel like I'm living in a board game."

"Sure... Jim," Mason said out of the corner of his mouth. No *uncle*. He pulled his hand out of Jim's grasp and dried it on the back of his pants. It was hard to believe that this man could still work up a sweat during a handshake after thirty years in sales.

"Please, please, have a seat. Amber tells me you're hoping to come back."

Amber had not taken it well when Mason had finally gotten around to telling her that he quit his job. Her reaction might not have been so severe, but he had forgotten all about telling her when they left the Farm. She found out two days later when she asked what time he would be home for dinner that night. Amber had given Mason a choice. He could either go back to work for Uncle Jim or find someone else to pay his bills when she left.

"We would love to have you back," Jim continued. "This interview, if you want to call it that, is just a formality. Gotta have something on file for HR just in case."

Right. *HR*. This was a man who did not have any managers or supervisors in his company because he preferred to micromanage everything. He *was* HR. And accounting. And sales and inventory and marketing. And any other department a used car dealership could possibly need.

"No problem," said Mason. He showed off his used-car smile out of habit, unsure of how effective it would be on the man who had taught it to him. Jim didn't seem to mind. He let out a sound that could be firmly placed somewhere between a chuckle and Santa Claus.

"Let's start with a tour. Make sure you remember the lay of the land."

Nothing had changed in the two years since he had been there other than the cars in the showroom. They walked through the lobby, past all of the plastic palm trees, out onto the lot. Mason stayed a step behind Jim as they walked, trying to avoid any unnecessary conversation.

After passing a couple rows of cars and waving to—or shaking hands with—everyone that they passed, Jim broke the silence.

"So? What do you think? I know it hasn't changed much since you left but if it ain't broke, don't fix it, am I right?"

For a moment, Mason considered telling Jim what he really thought about the idea of working there again. Then he remembered that he was there for Amber and put on his salesman face instead.

"Are you sure you didn't start selling new cars? Inventory looks great."

"Certified pre-owned. Every single one." Jim laughed. He was beaming like a new father talking about his first-born son.

"Well then, those boys over in detailing are doing a helluva job."

"Come on now, Mason, don't sound so surprised. You used to be one of those boys."

Uncle Jim's was the biggest used car lot in the state and it got that way because Jim did everything he could to make people forget that the cars he was selling were used. Detailing was the biggest department at the lot by a wide margin. When Mason first started working for Jim, he worked in detailing.

"Besides," Jim said, "nothing's really ever new, is it? It's always made of something used."

They headed back toward Jim's office to take care of the paperwork. As they got closer to the showroom doors, Mason could see a red ball sitting in front of the glass door. At first, he thought his eyes must be playing tricks on him, that it was just the reflection of the sun off of one of the taillights in the lot. The closer they got to it, the harder it was to keep fooling himself. It was a red tennis ball sitting in front of the door. *Weird coincidence.*

Somehow, Jim did not see the ball. If he had, there was no way he would not have picked it up. It was a blemish on the picture-perfect mirage he had built his dealership to be. Jim opened the door for Mason and the ball rolled between his legs toward the street.

They crossed the showroom to the office and Jim closed the door behind them as Mason sat down.

"Let's get right to it," Jim said as he pulled a folder out of his desk. "Should be pretty straightforward. Just a handful of questions and then a couple of forms."

Jim took a pen out of the *World's Best Boss* coffee mug that he undoubtedly bought himself and clicked the top several times.

"Okay. First question. Why did you leave your last job?"

Mason scratched the back of his neck and let out a nervous laugh.

"Funny you should ask because I—" *told them the same thing I told you when I quit.* That was how he was going to answer but he stopped when he heard a single knock on the office door. Then another. Then another.

"You what?" Jim ignored the knocking.

"I...uhh..." Another knock. "I told them..." And another. "What I said was..." And another.

Jim started clicking the pen again, still ignoring the knocking.

"Sorry," Mason said. He shook his head, trying to refocus himself. Another knock. "Are you going to check on that?"

"Check on what?"

Another knock. Mason jumped up from his chair and threw open the office door.

"On this." There was no one there. The showroom was empty. The receptionist was outside the main door on the other side of the room talking on her cell phone. But there *was* a red ball bouncing past one of the trucks on display.

"Is this some kind of a joke? Who is out there?" Mason yelled into the empty room.

Jim closed the folder and put it back in the desk drawer. He clicked the pen, set it down, and pushed himself to his feet.

"You can go now," he said to Mason and closed the office door in his face.

***

Mason had just finished setting the table and was pulling dinner out of the oven when Amber got home. Pot roast. It was his specialty. And his go-to when he knew he was going to be in trouble with Amber.

On a typical evening, Mason would know that she was home when Jacoby ran to the living room and jumped onto the couch to look out the window. His entire body wriggled with excitement as soon as Amber's car turned onto their street.

It wasn't a typical night. Jacoby had been glued to Mason's feet since they had left the asylum. Mason found out Amber was home when all of the cabinet doors in the kitchen rattled as the front door slammed closed.

"You must have had a good day," Mason said. He showed her the smile that he knew she could not resist.

"Are you kidding?" Apparently she could resist it. Amber tossed her keys on the kitchen counter next to Mason. "I went out on a limb for you. Told my uncle you were ready to commit this time. Begged him to give you another chance. What the hell is wrong with you? If you didn't want the job you should have just told me. You didn't have to pull that stunt to get out of it."

Jacoby finally left Mason's side. He cowered out of the kitchen and hid under the dining room table with his head under his paws and his ears pinned back.

"It wasn't a stunt. Someone is screwing with me."

"I don't want to hear it. My uncle is pissed. And honestly, so am I."

"Never would've guessed," Mason said.

"Don't."

"Seriously. Someone is messing with me. I thought it was just some stoner kids looking for a laugh at that asylum but whoever it was followed me to the lot and did it again."

"What are you talking about?" Amber was still yelling, but the edge in her voice softened a bit.

"That ball."

"What ball? We were the only ones at the Farm. And my uncle said you pretended to hear something and started yelling at an empty room."

"The red ball that kept showing up. Someone put it in the parking lot today and then kept bouncing it against the door during my interview."

"There was no ball! At the asylum or the car lot. You're just lazy. You didn't want the job I lined up for you. That's fine. But you can find someone else to mooch off of." With that Amber picked her keys up off of the counter and stormed out of the house.

3

Amber did not come home that night. Mason lay in bed staring at the ceiling with Jacoby's head resting on his chest. He mindlessly scratched behind Jacoby's ear as he replayed his fight with Amber in his head.

Maybe she was right. Jim clearly had not heard the ball bouncing against the door. If she didn't see the ball at the asylum, maybe there wasn't someone messing with him. It could be all in his head.

Jacoby did not fall asleep. Every time his eyes started to droop, he snapped his head up and scanned the room. He growled at each corner like he was tough, but kept his ears pulled back like he was terrified of the shadows.

Mason did not notice. He was too busy living in his head. He was imagining having to do the same thing every day for the next thirty years. And trying to figure out what his dog had been freaking out about in that cemetery. And thinking about wedding rings and diapers. And red tennis balls.

Eventually, Mason's hand stopped scratching Jacoby and just rested on the back of the dog's head. His eyelids relaxed and he drifted off to sleep.

***

His dream began with a ball—his ball—bouncing away from him. Mason laughed and ran after it. No matter how fast he went, it stayed just beyond his reach. He chased the ball through a field next to a stream and followed it into a forest. The sun was setting and the trees were thick. A group of children laughed somewhere in the forest. They sounded close. Mason stopped chasing the ball and looked around. Those kids sounded like they were having so much fun.

He could not see them anywhere, so he followed the sound. He was close. The laughter was deafening. Those kids must have been just around the next curve in the trail. But there was no one there and the laughter stopped. Mason looked around. Maybe they had seen him coming and decided to hide.

A squirrel climbed up a tree and scared a bird. It flapped its way to another treetop. Mason was alone.

The laughing started again but Mason was nowhere near where it was coming from. Confused, but not worried, Mason turned his attention back to catching his ball. He got back to where he had been when he first heard the laughter and—as if it had been waiting for him—he saw it bouncing down the trail just ahead.

It bounced off of a rock on the trail and between two trees. Mason turned and followed. The ball kept bouncing along without hitting any of the trees until suddenly all of the trees were gone.

Mason could almost reach it. The sun was most of the way down, but Mason found himself surrounded by light.

He was standing on a road. The light was coming from a truck speeding toward him. Mason could not move. He closed his eyes and braced for the impact.

Silence.

Blackness.

Then, the whine of a drill. A sharp pain in the side of his head. The silhouette of a young girl. Sunken eyes, greasy hair, blood dripping from holes on either side of her forehead, long sharp teeth.

His ball bounced down a dimly lit hallway.

Children laughed.

A dog barked.

The weight of the dog landed on his stomach.

Jacoby kept barking but moved off of Mason's stomach as he sat up. Mason was soaking wet, his heart pounding inside his ears.

Mason reached up and rubbed his forehead. It hurt, but there were no drill holes.

He hugged Jacoby.

"It was just a dream, buddy. All in my head."

Jacoby stopped barking but did not seem convinced. The barks were replaced by a low, guttural growl and he did not lean into Mason's side like he usually did when he got extra attention.

"Just a dream," Mason said again. "We're okay."

He pushed Jacoby over to Amber's empty side of the bed and checked his phone. No messages. He got out of bed and headed to the kitchen for a glass of water.

Mason filled a glass and let the faucet run while he drank. When the glass was empty, he refilled it and set it on the counter. A gust of wind rattled the window above the sink, sending a shudder through Mason's body. He splashed some water on his face and grabbed the dish towel that was hanging from the handle of the oven.

Mason dried his face and sipped the water as he walked into the living room. He looked out the window. The driveway was still empty. He checked his phone again—*one thirty-seven*. He checked that the doorknob on the front door was locked. It was.

He took another sip of water and started back toward the bedroom. Jacoby growled from the hallway. Something knocked against the door.

"Just in my head," Mason said. Then he turned back and locked the deadbolt.

4

"No. No way," Jeremy said as Mason parked his motorcycle and took off his helmet. "Boss said if you came back we're supposed to make you leave."

"Good to see you too, Jeremy."

"I'm serious. I can't let you go in there."

"How are you going to stop me?" Mason was already halfway from his parking spot to the showroom door. "Besides, you owe me. You wouldn't have even made it out of detailing if I hadn't vouched for you with Jim, remember?"

Mason reached for the door handle. Jeremy pressed his back against the door.

"Are you going to move or am I going to have to open this door through you?" Mason said.

Jeremy did not say anything. After a few seconds of staring each other down, he stepped aside.

"Good choice. And don't worry. If Jim asks, I never even saw you."

Mason threw the door open and marched across the showroom. By the time the receptionist recognized him, he was already at the door to Jim's office.

The office door was open but Mason still knocked on his way into the room. Jim was on the phone.

"I'll call you back." Jim set down the receiver. "What the hell are you doing here?" he asked Mason. There was no salesman smile this time.

"Hear me out, please. I messed up yesterday. I'm sorry." Mason went on to explain his experiences with the red ball, how he thought someone was messing with him. "Amber didn't come home last night so I had plenty of time to think. You know, we started talking about marriage and kids a while back and I think this whole thing with the ball was just the stress showing up in its own way. Like a mini-mental breakdown or something."

Jim did not look like he believed a word of it, but he grunted and nodded for Mason to continue.

"I panicked but didn't realize it, so my brain started playing tricks on me. In a way, I was right. Someone was messing with me. That someone just happened to be me."

Jim grunted again, waiting for the pitch.

"So anyway, I figured out what happened and I got it under control. I came back here to beg you to give me another chance."

Jim thought about it. The clock above the office door ticked. Mason felt like a kid in school waiting for the final few seconds to pass before the bell rang. *Tick. Tick. Tick.*

"You won't start out selling cars."

"That's perfectly fine." Mason smiled. "I don't mind starting over in detailing."

"Oh no. You won't be doing that either." Jim was smiling now too. "And you won't be getting paid until your trial period is over."

Mason raised an eyebrow, but he was desperate.

"What did you have in mind?"

***

Jim put Mason to work immediately after his apology speech. Mason had not been expecting that, but was in no position to argue. They left the office and Jim tossed him an old pair of coveralls and a brush.

"Start scrubbing."

"Scrubbing what?"

"Everything." Jim laughed and walked away.

Mason scrubbed all of the oil spots off of the floor in the shop. The grout and trim in the restrooms were spotless. The toilet bowls were clean enough to drink from. The tiles on the showroom floor were so thoroughly polished that they might as well have been mirrors.

"Not bad," Jim said. "Tomorrow morning you can start on the parking lot."

Mason managed to hold his tongue. He was already on thin ice with Amber, the last thing he needed was for her to get another call from Uncle Jim.

"Yes sir. See you in the morning."

"Six o'clock." Jim chuckled as he walked out of the dealership.

It was a quarter past nine when Mason pulled his bike into the driveway. His entire body ached and he was covered in grease and bleach. A light was on in the kitchen. Mason did not even bother with the kickstand. He jumped off the motorcycle and laid it on the side of the driveway as he ran inside.

Amber was in the kitchen with Jacoby. The dog came running when Mason opened the front door and leapt into his chest. On an ordinary day, Mason would have wrapped him in a hug before settling him down but after the day he had just had, Mason was lucky to even stay on his feet. Catching Jacoby out of the air was impossible when he could barely lift his own arms. Jacoby smacked into his chest and dropped to the floor. The Australian shepherd started hopping, trying to get high enough to lick Mason's face.

Amber followed Jacoby out of the kitchen, drying her hands with a dish towel. She noticed how exhausted Mason looked and smiled. She finished drying off her hands and set the towel on the back of the couch.

"Hey." She dragged Jacoby down the hallway by the collar and closed him in the bedroom.

When Amber got back to the living room, Mason collapsed into her arms.

"I'm so glad you are back," he whispered. He did not have the energy to speak louder. "I messed up. But I'm trying."

As he spoke, something knocked against the front door. Jacoby started barking and scratching to be let out of the bedroom. Mason ignored it.

"I'll always keep trying."

5

After their walk together to the nurse's office, Mason and Amber became inseparable.

At recess, they made up games or went on adventures together. Mason usually suggested that they play *Ghostbusters*. He loved the theme song and sang it as they ran around the playground. Plus, it gave him extra opportunities to tease Amber about the "ghost" in her dining room. They ate lunch together every day, sitting side-by-side rather than across from each other. That way, it was easier to trade food and eat off of each other's trays.

On the first day of Christmas break during fourth grade, Amber walked over to Mason's house. She knocked on the front door. Mason's dad answered.

"Hello Mr. Turlock," she said, "I was hoping to invite Mason over for dinner at my house tonight. My family is going to visit relatives for the holidays, so after tomorrow I won't be able to see him again until we go back to school."

Mason's dad laughed.

"Come on in," he said. "He's in his room. Up the stairs on the right. It's all right with me but you'll have to ask him."

"Okay," Mason said when Amber invited him over, "on one condition. You have to introduce me to your ghost." Mason grabbed his hat and raced Amber down the stairs. "And when he doesn't show up, you have to admit that ghosts aren't real."

Amber's house was only a mile and a half from Mason's, but it took them a full hour to get there. They passed a snowbank piled up at the end of a driveway. Mason tackled Amber into the snow. She retaliated by chasing him down and dropping a handful of snow down the back of his coat, which every kid knew was an act of war.

After a lengthy snowball battle, they continued toward her house until they saw another snowbank and the whole thing started over again.

By the time they finally got to Amber's house, their clothes were soaked, their faces were bright red and chapped from the cold, and their cheeks hurt from laughing too much.

Amber stomped her boots on the porch and went inside.

"Wait here. Take off your boots and coat. I'll go get us some towels."

Mason stood just outside the open door, stomping his boots, trying to brush all of the loose snow from his jacket and pants. Amber's mom walked around the corner, her blonde hair pulled back into a messy bun. She wore a reindeer apron over her red Christmas sweater. The sleeves were rolled up to her elbows. She wiped her hands on the apron. Her forehead glistened with a thin layer of sweat from spending the day in front of a hot stove. A single streak of flour stuck to her cheek.

Mason quit stomping. His eyes widened and he stood bolt upright, just like his cousin had told him soldiers are supposed to do when they see their boss—or a pretty girl.

"You must be Mason. Dinner is just about ready. I hope you like dumplings." Her teeth looked big when she smiled. But not too big. And they were as white as the snow he had spent the last hour throwing at her daughter.

"Yes ma'am, I am," Mason replied, trying to keep up the good soldier act. "I've never had dumplings before."

"I'll tell you what... if you don't like them, I can whip up something else for you."

"That won't be necessary. They smell great. Besides, I'm mostly here to prove to Amber that ghosts don't exist."

"Is that right?" Amber's mom laughed. A timer dinged in the kitchen.

Mason watched her go until he was hit in the face with a bath towel. Amber had already dried herself off and changed into dry clothes. She was wearing her own red sweater and had put her own blonde hair into a bun. The spitting image of her mother.

"Do you need any help, Mom?"

Amber's mom poked her head out of the kitchen.

"Not right now. You kids go have some fun. But in about twenty minutes you could come set the table."

"No problem," Mason said, though she had clearly been talking to Amber.

"Thank you, Mason. That's very sweet. And maybe you'll see your ghost before dinner so you can enjoy the food." She winked at him and returned to her spot in front of the oven. Mason turned as red as Amber's sweater.

Mason and Amber went up the stairs to Amber's room to get supplies for their ghost hunt.

"We need cards," Amber said. "He loves games. He can't play them but he likes to watch."

"Got 'em." Mason held up a deck.

"And my doll." Amber took a two-foot tall doll from the closet. "And her hairbrush."

"Why? What kind of weirdo ghost are we dealing with?"

"He's not a weirdo. He had a daughter and he misses her. Seeing me play with my doll reminds him of her."

"Did he tell you that? I thought he never talked to you."

"Well... no. I'm just assuming."

"And I'm assuming he's a weirdo who wants to possess you. *If* he even exists. Which he doesn't."

They spent a few more minutes grabbing random things from Amber's room to use as ghost bait. The last thing Amber picked up was her Polaroid camera. They went back downstairs toward the dining room. Amber slowed as they passed the open bathroom door.

"Oh. A candle. He likes vanilla." She took the candle from the back of the toilet.

In the dining room, Amber took the centerpiece off of the table and told Mason to turn off the light. She dealt the cards for a game of solitaire and set her doll in one of the chairs. Amber put the camera strap around her neck and laid the other trinkets around the table.

"Do you want to play cards or brush Becky's hair?" She held out the hairbrush to Mason. He sat down in front of the cards. "Mom?" Amber called into the kitchen. "Could you come light the candle for us, please?"

Her mother came in with a book of matches.

"Good luck," she said.

Amber started brushing her doll's hair. Mason was cruising through his game of solitaire. Neither of them said a word.

Mason felt a chill, just for a moment. The flame of the candle wavered. He looked over his shoulder to see if someone had opened the front door or a window or something. But the only other person in the house was Amber's mom and he could hear the oven door creak in the kitchen as she opened it.

Amber was still brushing Becky's hair but she had one hand on the camera and a smile was spreading across her face.

Mason looked around the dining room. Amber noticed and whisper-yelled at him.

"Keep playing. You'll scare him away."

Mason scrunched up his face at her, but went back to his game. There was no one there to scare off. They were alone. Amber's camera flashed.

"I told you! I told you!"

"Told me what? There's nothing there," Mason said, though he could not be sure. He was still rubbing the stars out of his eyes.

"Albert," Amber said, ignoring Mason, "this is my friend Mason. He doesn't think you are real."

"You're talking to the wall," Mason said.

"No, wait. Please. Don't go." Then Amber turned back to Mason. "Why would you say that? You scared him away."

"Scared who? Albert? How do you know that is his name if he never talks? You're making this all up."

"Am not!"

"Then how do you know that's his name?"

"That's just what I call him. He likes it."

"No way," Mason said. "*Ghosts. Aren't. Real.*"

"Yes they are. Here, look." Amber finished shaking the Polaroid picture and handed it to Mason.

"This is a picture of the wall..."

"No. Look. Right there." She pointed to a white spot in the photo.

"It's a wall," Mason said.

They argued about it all through dinner, which Mason ate three helpings of, and both even tried to convince Amber's mom to take their side. Mason had to give her mom credit, she knew how to stay neutral.

Amber's mom brought out a plate of cookies and two glasses of milk. She left them to their debate while she cleaned up the kitchen. That was at *six-fifteen*. Amber's step-dad got home from work at *eight-thirty*. All that remained of the cookies were a few crumbs. Both glasses of milk were long gone. But their debate raged on.

Amber's father had died before her second birthday. Her mom remarried two years later. The man that she married had been a friend of Amber's parents and wanted to make it clear that he was not trying to replace her father, so he asked that Amber call him Uncle Jim instead of dad.

"Uncle Jim! Uncle Jim! Come look at this picture," Amber yelled before the front door closed behind him. Jim walked over to the table and introduced himself to Mason.

"Yeah, yeah. You're Uncle Jim. He's Mason. Here, look. You see it right? Right?" She shoved the photo into Jim's face. He leaned back and took it.

"Yes, Amber," he said, "I see it. You took a picture of the wall."

"Ha! I told you. I'm right."

Amber snatched the picture away from her step-father and gave him the same look she had given Mason when he pulled the chair out from under her on the first day of school.

"You really don't see him? He's right there."

"Who is, Amber?" Uncle Jim asked.

"Albert. Look." She pointed at the white spot in the photograph.

Jim took the snapshot from her again and pretended to study it.

"Ahh. Mmhmm. You know, now that you mention it, I think I do see him. Hard to tell for sure though." He winked at Mason and handed the picture back to Amber. Mason laughed. Uncle Jim did not stay neutral nearly as well as Amber's mom did.

Amber's mom had been on the phone in the kitchen when Jim came in. She hung up and entered the dining room.

"Mason, I just spoke with your parents. Since we lost track of time tonight, I can give you a ride home now or you can stay until after breakfast in the morning."

"Stay," Amber answered for him. She turned to Mason. "Please?"

"Sure," he said. "You still think ghosts are real even though I am obviously right. Maybe by morning I'll have you convinced."

"Okay," Amber's mom said, "but you better convince her quickly. We are going to have to get to bed in the next hour or so."

The kids raced up to Amber's room to continue their debate, both still convinced that the picture Amber had taken proved them right.

"Agree to disagree," Mason said after another ten minutes of arguing. He did not really understand what it meant but his dad always said it to his mom when he got tired of trying to convince her she was wrong. It seemed appropriate. *Everyone* knows ghosts are not real. Except Amber. She's crazy.

"Fine. Want to play a game?"

She went into her closet and grabbed *Mouse Trap.* In a matter of seconds, they forgot all about their argument and were just two best friends playing a game together like nothing happened.

Amber's mom came into the room a short while later to let them know it was time for bed. She gave a pillow and two blankets to Mason—one to lay on the floor and one to lie under.

"Lights out," she said. "We are leaving early in the morning and I don't want to have to fight to wake you up."

As soon as her mom left the room, Amber turned on the lamp next to her bed.

"Mason? Are you going to sleep?"

"Isn't that what we are supposed to be doing?" He looked up at her from his makeshift bed on the floor.

Amber said nothing, climbed out of her bed, and stretched out next to him on the floor. After a minute of staring up at the ceiling, she rolled onto her side to face him.

"I'm going to miss you," she said.

Mason rolled onto his side as well but did not say anything. They stared into each other's eyes for what was either ten seconds or half the night. Mason smiled. She turned her head away from him and tucked her ear to her shoulder.

Mason scooted himself a little closer to her. Then Amber smiled. She knew what was going to happen before Mason did. She had seen it often enough on TV. He licked his lips lightly and stretched his neck toward her. He had not moved close enough, so Amber met him halfway. He closed his eyes and leaned in. It was meant to be a quick peck on her lips but he missed and got the tip of her nose instead.

When Mason rolled back away from her, Amber could see how red his face was, even in the dim yellow light from the lamp. But Mason was determined to play it cool, staring straight up with one hand behind his head.

“Don’t worry,” he said. “I’ll be here when you get back.”

Amber rolled closer, hoping he would try their first kiss again. Mason did not notice—and didn’t know he had missed—and kept talking.

“And even if something crazy happens, I can always come haunt you like Albert.”

Amber slugged him in the shoulder and climbed back into her bed.

“You’re such a jerk,” she said, laughing.

6

Two weeks. That was how long Mason's trial period at the car lot was supposed to last. Two weeks of never-ending grunt work, of doing anything and everything Jim could think of to make him give up. Two weeks of scrubbing toilets and cleaning air ducts and scrubbing ten-year-old grease stains off of the concrete floor in the shop. Two weeks of fourteen-hour days. Two weeks of sweeping dust off of a parking lot that was surrounded on all sides by dirt fields.

Two weeks of watching a red ball roll across the floor even though he was the only person in the room. Two weeks of hearing that ball bouncing in the hallway while he was trying to sleep.

Two weeks of Jacoby being clingy and skittish. Two weeks of not being able to say a word of it to Amber out of fear that she would leave again—and for good.

Two weeks of trying to convince himself that it really was all in his head.

Agree to disagree.

***

Jim called Mason into his office at *four-thirty* on Friday. It was the last day of his tryout. Mason had managed to limit his responses to *yes sir, no sir, thank you, sir* through all of it.

"I'm impressed," Jim said when Mason entered the office. "I thought for sure you'd have cracked by now. You must really be serious about coming back."

"Yes sir."

"Congrats. You've passed every test I could think of. Why don't you go ahead and take off a little early today. First thing Monday morning, you'll be back out on sales."

"Thank you, sir." Mason turned to leave, holding back a smile until Jim could no longer see his face.

"Oh, just one more thing," Jim said as Mason reached for the door. "I'll need you here tomorrow and Sunday. The boys over in detailing are taking the weekend off. You'll be covering for them."

Mason turned around. Jim was smirking behind the desk.

"All of them are off?"

"That's right. That's not going to be a problem for you, is it Mason?"

They watched each other in silence for several seconds, neither one blinking.

"No sir," Mason said finally, through clenched teeth.

***

Detailing was always done at the garage two miles up the road from the actual car lot. *Can't let them see how the sausage is made.* That's how Jim always explained it.

If Mason was going to be stuck working all weekend, at least he would not have to pretend to enjoy it. There were no customers or coworkers to put on a show for at the garage.

Mason had finished three cars, and was halfway through scrubbing the dashboard in the fourth, when that red tennis ball bounced against the windshield. The thud made him jump and he smashed his head into the panoramic sunroof.

Mason climbed out of the car, rubbing the back of his head. The sound of the door closing echoed throughout the empty garage. The ball hit him in the middle of his back. He screamed, more out of surprise than from pain—although a line-drive to the spine did not feel great.

Someone laughed.

It reminded Mason of the laughing kids in his dream. The ball rolled to a stop next to the front left tire of the 2012 Chevy Tahoe that he had been working on.

"That's it," Mason yelled. "This ends now. Whatever sick joke you're playing. It's over."

The laughter stopped. The garage was silent. He picked up the ball. Its fuzz squelched in his hand and a dark green slime oozed between his fingers. Mason walked across the garage. He put the ball into the saddlebag on his motorcycle, detached the bag from the bike, and threw it over his shoulder. It was his proof. Proof that someone was doing this to him, that it was not all in his head. He was not going to let it out of his sight.

Mason finished the Tahoe and three more cars before calling it a day, checking the saddlebag every couple of minutes to make sure that the ball was still there. It was. He kept it strapped to his shoulder as he rode home.

Since he had picked up the ball, he felt vindicated. It couldn't be in his head if he had the ball. And, a part of him—an admittedly irrational part—believed that whoever was doing this to him would have to stop now that they had been found out.

Riding home that evening was the first time since taking Amber to the Farm that Mason smiled. And not the fake smile he had been using with Jim for two weeks, it was genuine. His head was floating.

He had been right all along. And he could not wait to prove to Amber that he was not a nut job. It would take some doing, but this was not like their ghost debates. This time he could prove it.

As Mason walked from the driveway to the front door, he was giddy. He might as well have been six years old, skipping around on a playground. His hand never left the saddlebag on his shoulder as he went inside to the kitchen.

Amber was taking a roast out of the oven. Mason walked up behind her and wrapped his arms around her waist. He waited until she set the roast down on the counter, then leaned in and kissed her just in front of her ear.

"I have something to show you," he whispered as he pulled his face back from the side of her head and turned her around.

"Can we eat first? I'm glad you're in a good mood, but dinner is ready. It'll get cold." She thought he was trying to be romantic.

"No. Not that," he said. "Well... maybe that, later. I'm talking about this." Mason swung the saddlebag off of his shoulder and set it on the counter next to the roast.

As he unlatched the bag and opened the flap, a stream of thick, black water trickled out of the bag toward the food. Mason's face looked like a kid's on Christmas morning. He reached his hand into the bag to grab the ball.

Nothing.

"It was right here. I had it all day. It has to be here."

"What was?" Amber turned to the cupboard to take out a couple of plates, only half-listening.

"That damn red ball." Mason picked the bag up off of the counter and turned it over. A pen, forty-seven cents, a coffee stand punch card, and a pocket knife fell to the kitchen floor. He shook the bag. Nothing else came out.

He stuck his hand into the bag. It felt like he was digging through Jello that had not quite finished setting, but there was no ball. All of the pressure that had lifted on his way home came back, like someone was taking a power drill to his brain.

Amber looked worried. She had been so proud of him during the past two weeks, the way he had matured and stepped up his work ethic, even though she knew Uncle Jim had been making his life miserable to try to show her that Mason would never change. He had fully committed to his job at the car lot and it gave her hope that he might be close to committing to other things as well. But if he cracked under the pressure, he would be right back where he was two weeks ago.

"Maybe you should go lie down." Amber tried not to let the agitation show in her voice.

"No. No, I'm fine. I had that ball though. Someone threw it at my back in the garage earlier. I put it in here to show you. I had it on me all day. It doesn't make any sense."

"We talked about this already. That thing with the ball was all in your head. We were past all this, weren't we?"

"I was wrong. I mean... I was right, then I was wrong. Look." He pulled up his shirt to show her where the ball hit him. It still hurt when he leaned back against anything so there would have to be a mark or a bruise. Something.

"I don't see anything," Amber said. "I think we should go talk to someone. I'm going to call around and make us an appointment. For now, can we forget about the ball and just have dinner?"

***

Before Mason left for work on Monday morning, Amber helped him with his tie, kissed him, and wished him good luck. He forced a smile and headed to the car lot.

Everything went smoothly until just after lunch. On his way back out of the showroom, he passed Jeremy helping a family buy a minivan. There were two boys, maybe five and eight years old, who had made up a game to play while their parents were signing the paperwork. Mason smiled and waved to them as he walked past.

The red ball sailed past his ear. It bounced off the door and was headed straight for his face. He avoided a direct hit but the red fuzz grazed his cheek on its way by. The young boys started laughing. Mason raced out of the building before the ball had a chance to come at him again.

Mason gathered himself after the door closed behind him. He looked around. No one seemed to have noticed anything. Jim was in his office. The receptionist was on the phone trying to calm down a customer whose Tahoe had been given back to him with a cracked sunroof. Jeremy was clicking his pen, telling his customers to *sign here* and *initial there*. Their two boys were chasing each other around the showroom, laughing with each other, not at Mason.

There was no sign of a red tennis ball anywhere. For that he was grateful. But it was real and he knew it, even if nobody believed him. The cracks were starting to show. His heart had been racing for days. He had dark circles around his eyes, couldn't sit or stand without twitching, and he was unable to maintain eye contact with anyone for more than a second or two before his eyes darted around, looking for the ball or whoever might be the one throwing it.

***

Mason met Amber at the therapist's office after work on Tuesday. She made them an appointment for couple's counseling, claiming that it was the fastest way to get in as a new patient. While that may have been true, Mason did not like it. As far as he was concerned, the only problem with their relationship was that Amber thought he was either lying or crazy. And a couple's therapist was not going to get her to believe him.

Amber waited on the sidewalk in front of the building. A group of kids were playing basketball across the street. Every dribble made Mason twitch, looking for that little red ball. Amber leaned forward to kiss him when he walked up but the basketball bounced off of the rim at the same time. Mason jumped back.

"Let's just get this over with, okay?" he said.

Dr. Phillips was a just-over-middle-aged woman, short and round. She wore thick rimmed, semi-circle glasses that were much too big for her face and had to push them up the bridge of her nose every time she moved her head. She introduced herself to Mason and Amber with a smile as rehearsed as Mason's own. *Shrinks and salesmen are probably the only ones who can perfect that sort of smile.*

"Please," she said, "have a seat." She looked down at her notepad. "Amber, why don't you start by telling me what brought you here today?"

Amber pressed her lips together and tilted her head. She said nothing at first. Dr. Phillips folded her hands in her lap. Mason's eyes narrowed as he watched Amber, waiting for her response.

Amber began by telling the therapist that Mason had been seeing and hearing things. She said that he *thought* somebody was following him around trying to screw up his life. The woman across the room scribbled something on her notepad and urged Amber to continue. After Amber finished telling her version of the past month, the therapist nodded and made a sound that was closer to a grunt than a word.

"So that's pretty much it," Amber said.

"Okay, great," the therapist said, "now I would like you to tell me why *you* are here."

"I just told you."

"No, Amber. You told me what Mason has been dealing with, not why you felt that it called for a couple's session."

Amber looked quickly at Mason. He raised a hand toward the therapist, telling her to go ahead. He managed to hold back his laughter, but could not keep a smile from stretching across his lips.

"You had the first opening," she said.

"That is one possibility."

"I'm just trying to help him," Amber barked. The smile on Mason's face stretched wider.

"I believe you," Dr. Phillips said, "but is that really the only reason that you are here?"

Amber looked at Mason again. Teardrops clung to her eyelashes before falling down her cheeks. She turned back to the doctor.

"It's my fault."

Mason's eyes widened.

"No," he said. "How could this possibly be your fault?"

"Mason, let her finish," the doctor said.

"It is," Amber said to Mason. "I've been pushing you. We talked about getting married and having kids. You don't want that, but I kept bringing it up." The tears were flowing freely now.

"That has nothing to do with this," Mason said. "We are here because you don't believe me about that damn ball."

"There is no ball, Mason," Amber screamed at him. "No one is following you around. It's me. The ball is our future. You don't want it, but I keep throwing it at you anyway."

Dr. Phillips watched silently, taking notes, until an alarm went off on her phone. She swiped her finger across the screen to silence it.

"That was very good, you two. You touched on some very deep issues. Impressive for the first session. Going forward, I would like us to get together twice a week. But before you come back, I have some homework for you. I want you to leave..."

She paused long enough to confuse Mason and Amber. They looked at each other and stood up from their chairs. The therapist put on her smile again and told them to sit back down.

"That's not what I meant," she said with a chuckle. "I want you to leave town. Just the two of you." *She's good*, Mason thought. "It doesn't matter where you go, but go together, just the two of you. And no phones."

***

Mason was glad that they did not have to ride together when they left their appointment. It did not take long to get home, but he needed that time alone to digest everything Amber had said during the last hour.

He turned onto Evergreen Boulevard, a block before the freeway, so he could take the long way home. The street was appropriately named. It wound through five miles of forest alongside the river before reaching the edge of their neighborhood.

As soon as Mason rounded the first curve and was out of sight of the main road, he pulled over. He took off his helmet and buckled it to the side of the seat. He sighed and ran a hand through his hair.

He had tried to listen to Amber—really listen—without getting defensive. She was only trying to tell him how she felt about him, about their relationship, their future. *Obviously their future was together. She* had *to know that. They had been together since they were nine years old. He did not want that to change. But the labeling and planning? Was that necessary? Couldn't they just keep living their lives and see what happened?*

Mason's mouth began to water. His vision blurred. With one hand on the tire, he doubled over behind his Valkyrie and vomited on the side of the road.

A red-violet dusk was spreading across the sky. Mason looked up, breathing heavily. A stream of clouds drifted across the horizon. The wind blew from the trees toward the river. With it came the sound of laughing children.

Mason turned toward the sound and saw a ball bounce out of the trees. It settled at his feet. He picked it up and screamed as he threw it. It splashed into the water just over halfway across the river. Mason jumped back onto his motorcycle and rode toward home.

A boy stood by the trees holding a baseball glove. He watched Mason race off and yelled something, but the sound never caught up to the bike. Another boy emerged from the trees holding a bat.

"What's taking so long?" the second boy asked.

The first boy threw his arm up in the direction of Mason's speeding motorcycle.

"Some jackass threw our ball into the river."

During the ten minute ride through the trees, wind blowing through his hair, eyes squinting into the sunset, Mason's anger subsided. When he parked in the driveway, he wiped tears—partly from the wind, partly from realizing that Amber had a point—from the corners of his eyes. He had commitment issues and he probably *did* need to do a little growing up. He promised himself that he would at least make an effort with the therapy, though he would never admit it to her.

7

Amber folded a sweatshirt and put it in the duffel bag on the bed.

"Are you sure you want to do this?" she asked. "You just got out of the doghouse with Uncle Jim. Taking three days off in the middle of your first week might not be the best idea."

Mason walked up behind her and wrapped his arms around her waist.

"I'm sure. It's something that we need to do. For us. That's always a good idea."

She leaned back into him and reached up behind his neck to pull him closer. They stayed that way for almost a minute and then finished packing in silence, stopping occasionally to look at each other and smile.

Mason took the tent down from the top shelf in the hallway closet and loaded it, with their bag, into the trunk of Amber's car. Amber brought Jacoby out of the house on his leash and put him in the backseat.

"I thought the doctor said it had to be just us?" Mason said as he closed the trunk.

"Oh come on," Amber said. "He's a part of us. Besides, Jacoby loves camping."

The campground was twenty miles out of town along Highway 63. They had the road entirely to themselves because they were going at ten o'clock on a Wednesday morning. The campground was empty for the same reason—or because it was the middle of October and people were pretty much done camping for the year. Either way was fine by Mason. He had never been a big fan of other people.

They got to the campground just before noon. Amber started a fire to cook some burgers for lunch. Mason threw a stick for Jacoby to chase and worked on setting up the tent. The sound of the river crashing against the dock carried through the trees and into their campsite. The fire popped and crackled, flaring up with a hiss whenever a drop of grease fell from the hamburger patties.

Mason finished putting up the tent and sat down next to Amber. He reached over and rested his hand on top of hers. They smiled at each other. Before either of them said anything, Jacoby ran back with a stick—not the one Mason had thrown for him—and crashed into Mason's arm when he slid in the rocky dirt surrounding the fire pit instead of stopping. Mason and Amber broke out in laughter. Mason took the stick and waved it in front of Jacoby as he walked him over to the open part of the campsite to keep playing.

Mason threw the stick. Jacoby sprinted a couple of laps around the campsite before picking it up and bringing it halfway back to Mason. Then he dropped the stick and brought a pinecone instead. Mason threw the pinecone and Jacoby did the same thing with it, switching the pinecone for the original stick on his way back. Mason laughed and patted Jacoby on the head.

Amber called to him a few minutes later when their lunch was ready. Mason threw the stick down toward the river and jogged back to his seat next to her. Jacoby raced toward the water.

"You're having fun," Amber said. Mason couldn't tell if that was a statement or a question.

"It's nice to be able to just block everything else out for a while. Right now, it's just us. I like that."

They ate their hamburgers, enjoying the stillness of the trees around them until Jacoby came back. He had jumped into the river to grab a different stick and his fur was soaked. He trotted up between them, dropped the stick and shook. Drops of river water covered Mason, Amber, and their lunches. They started laughing again. Mason tore a piece of meat from his burger and tossed it to Jacoby. The three of them ate in silence around the fire.

That night, Mason had the dream with the ball again. As he chased it through the trees, he heard laughter but did not follow it. Instead he focused on the ball. *His ball.* Just as it bounced out of the woods toward the road, he caught it. Standing on the shoulder of the roadway, Mason held his prize up in the moonlight as a blue pickup raced by less than three feet from where he was standing.

Amber and Mason slept until the sun was almost directly overhead. They would have stayed bundled up in their sleeping bags longer—it was only forty-two degrees despite the sun—but Jacoby started pawing at the zipper of the tent and whimpering. Amber groaned. She rolled over and shook Mason's shoulder.

"Okay, okay. I'm going," he said as he crawled out of the sleeping bag.

The brightness of the sunlight when Mason unzipped the tent knocked him back enough that he had to use his other hand to keep from falling onto Amber. He blinked hard and squinted his way out of the tent. Jacoby was halfway to the river before Mason finished rubbing the last of the sleep from his eyes.

Jacoby was practically skipping, or as close to it as a dog can get, along the riverbank. After several minutes of racing back and forth from the water to the trees, Jacoby remembered why he needed out of the tent. Mason skipped rocks while he waited for Jacoby to pick a tree. He glanced back at the tent. Amber was just crawling out of it. He threw another rock across the top of the water and smiled. He could stay out here with Amber forever, just the two of them and Jacoby. That would be pretty much perfect.

Jacoby bounded up to Mason at the same time as the sound of splitting wood. He decided that he had some time to play with Jacoby by the water while Amber built a fire.

Mason walked up to the treeline to find a good stick to throw for his dog. He blinked as he bent down to grab one. A scene from his dream flashed on the inside of his eyelids. *A red ball bouncing through the trees and he—arms outstretched—laughing while chasing after it.* Mason picked up the stick and opened his eyes. He shook his head to rid himself of the image.

Jacoby jumped up, trying to take the stick from Mason before he had a chance to throw it. Mason raised it up over his head, but Jacoby kept trying, hopping on his hind legs. Finally, Mason quit teasing the dog and threw the stick. It spun end over end and landed about twenty feet out in the water. The current near the campground was slow—a good thing since it was full of children from May to September every year. *Who knows how many would have ended up missing if it were stronger?*

Mason walked toward the water after he threw the stick. He did not get far before Jacoby dropped the stick at his feet. As soon as Mason bent down to grab it, Jacoby decided to dry himself off. Water from his fur sprayed Mason's face. He spat out the drops that had landed in his mouth and scratched behind Jacoby's ears.

"You had that planned the whole time, didn't you?" he said through clenched teeth, feigning anger. "Yes you did." Mason picked up the stick and stood up. "Come on, buddy. Let's go see what your mom's got going on."

Amber was struggling to get the fire started. The paper plate that she had lit burnt out without catching any of the wood on fire. Mason handed her the stick.

"I'll trade you," he said.

She leaned forward to kiss Mason but hesitated.

"You smell like wet dog."

"Take it up with him." Mason cocked a thumb at Jacoby, who was squirming with anticipation, trying to figure out which one of them was going to throw his stick.

Amber jogged off with Jacoby, leaving Mason to tend to the fire, which amounted to little more than blackened kindling and ash that used to be paper plates. There were no visible embers but the ashes were still smoking. Mason leaned down to rearrange the wood and start over. Some sap on one of the sticks was finally hot enough to pop. It shot straight into Mason's eye. He yelled out and threw his hands to his face.

Behind closed eyelids, Mason could see the ember that had landed in his eye, an orange speck surrounded by blackness. He squeezed his eyes tighter and rubbed the one that had been hit, as if that would undo the searing pain. The orange speck darkened and moved around as he rubbed. The dark orange became red—a bright red ball—and bounced around behind his closed eyelid.

Amber heard his scream and sprinted back to the campsite. She grabbed a bottle of water from the cooler, forced his eyes open, and poured the water directly into them.

"Thanks," Mason said, spraying the water that had run down into his mouth at the fire pit.

"Maybe we should call it," Amber said. "We could just have a quiet night at home."

"No. I'm fine. This was what you wanted to do. And it's nice having the whole place to ourselves. Really, I'm fine."

"Are you sure?"

"Yes." Mason looked at the wet fire pit. "I don't think we are going to get this started anytime soon, though." He flashed her his work smile and the debate was over. They would stay at the campsite for another night.

They spent the afternoon walking along the riverbank, playing keep-away with Jacoby, holding hands. They did not talk much, but they did not need to.

When the sun went down, they skipped dinner and instead feasted on roasted marshmallows and chocolate—a s'mores-gasbord, Mason called it. They curled up on a blanket next to the fire. The night was cold and clear and Amber was convinced that there was supposed to be a meteor shower.

"Make a wish," she said as one moved across the sky above their heads.

"Okay," Mason said. "I wish that airplane lands on-time so no one is late for anything."

"You just know how to take the fun out of everything, don't you?" Amber shoved his arm and kissed his cheek.

"It's what I'm here for."

They stayed there, looking up at the stars watching meteors—or airplanes—cross the sky, until the fire burnt itself out. Jacoby was the first to fall asleep.

"Do you think that shrink was right?" Mason asked Amber as she started to drift off.

"About what?" she said, yawning as she spoke.

"About us. Is there something wrong here? Are we okay?"

"We will be," Amber said through another yawn. "As long as we are honest with each other, we will be."

Mason had one hand folded underneath his head with the other wrapped around Amber's shoulder. He knew the conversation was over when she turned and buried her face into his armpit. By then, Jacoby had rolled onto his back and fell asleep with his tongue hanging out of his mouth and all four of his paws in the air, like a bad stage actor performing a death scene.

Amber snored lightly. She loved being outdoors but it always made her a bit congested. The snoring was soft enough that Mason could spin it as endearing, and it was never loud enough to keep him from being able to fall asleep himself. He tucked his chin down and kissed the top of her head.

"Thank you," he whispered. "We needed this."

It was another hour before the fire burnt itself out. Mason let his mind wander, mesmerized by the stars.

Maybe it wouldn't be so bad to plan out their future. He'd never wanted to be tied down, but tied or not, he wasn't going anywhere. He had been with Amber forever. There was no reason to think that would change anytime soon. And kids? Don't people say getting a dog is like a trial run for having kids? Having Jacoby had been great—training, feeding, playing, the excitement every time he came home—would having a kid really be so different?

The last flame flickered out with a pop. All that remained were a few glowing orange clumps surrounded by ash. Mason nudged Amber and told her it was time to call it a night. She took Jacoby to the tent.

Mason took the pot from the picnic table over to the water spigot and filled it. A cloud of ash shot up as he poured the water into the fire pit. It let out a loud hiss as the last of the embers were extinguished.

Jacoby started to growl.

Mason crawled into the sleeping bag and turned off his lantern. Jacoby stretched out across his shins but did not lay his head down. He was still growling when Mason fell asleep.

As he drifted off, Mason found himself back in that same never-ending forest. The sun was going down and his ball kept bouncing away from him, just out of reach. Laughter swirled through the trees. He felt six years old again and nothing mattered except catching his ball. No stress, no worries, just the thrill of the chase.

The ball bounced around a tree. As he turned to follow it into the shadow of the tree trunk, a figure appeared in the darkness. A girl. Long, wet hair, holes on the sides of her head, just in front of her ears, blood smeared and dried around her lips. Mason jumped backward trying not to run into her. He lost his footing and stumbled. He reached out and grabbed the tree to keep from falling to the ground.

The girl was gone. The ball bounced in the exact spot she had been standing. Mason forgot about the girl and ran after the ball. He started laughing as it moved down the trail just fast enough to stay out of reach.

He was going to catch it. Mason reached out, leaned forward, stretched his fingers. He could almost touch it. He loaded his weight into his legs and dove forward.

Before he could close his hand around the ball something knocked him back, taking the air out of him as it did. He woke up in his sleeping bag, struggling to catch his breath. It felt like he had an anvil sitting on his chest. Not an anvil, a seventy pound dog.

Mason was sweating like he had *actually* been running through the trees instead of just dreaming about it. He tried to pull in a breath but Jacoby's weight kept his lungs from expanding. He reached up with a grunt and shoved the dog far enough toward his waist so that he was able to breathe. His hands sunk into something wet. *God-damn dog pissed on me,* he thought. He pulled his hands back and the wetness stuck to them like syrup. Jacoby did not move. Mason bolted upright and shook Jacoby.

"Jacoby! Wake up," he yelled.

He kept shaking the dog. Amber sat up next to him.

"What are you—"

"Turn on the lantern," Mason said to her. "Jacoby? Jacoby!"

The light from the lantern spread throughout the tent. Amber saw it first. Her mouth fell open and her hands rose to catch her scream. Mason's hands were covered in Jacoby's blood. There was a golf ball–sized hole in his neck, fur matted around the hole. His blood pooled around his limp body on top of the sleeping bag.

Mason scrambled out from underneath his dead dog, trying not to disturb the body more than he already had. As Mason shimmied toward the back of the tent, Jacoby's body rolled off of him. The blood—combined with the slick surface of the sleeping bag—created a makeshift slip-n-slide. Jacoby's body slid across the tent.

Mason rushed over to unzip the tent. Jacoby's weight landing on his chest had been what woke him up. Whoever had done this could not have gone very far. But the tent was zipped and he had not heard the zipper. *Who would take the time to close the tent after killing a dog?* Mason pushed the thought from his mind and focused on catching the person who did it—probably the same person who had been messing with him all along.

He crawled out into the darkness of the campground and got to his feet, ready to run around blindly in the dark. Then he thought better of it. He reached back into the tent and took the lantern. Amber did not even notice that the light was gone. She wouldn't mind. She could cry for Jacoby in the dark. There was no need for her to keep staring at Jacoby's lifeless body.

Mason held up the lantern and looked around the campsite, hoping to see something that would show him which way they went. The campground was still. No footprints, no twigs breaking or gravel shifting under somebody's fleeing feet. As far as Mason could tell, there was no one else for miles. A cold gust of wind blew up from the river. Mason shivered and rubbed his shoulders. He turned back to get Amber out of the tent. He bent down with the lantern. The light reflected in Jacoby's open eyes. Black mirrors. The dog's lips were parted, teeth bared. The pool of blood on the sleeping bag was beginning to congeal. More black. Mason gagged and turned his head away from the tent.

The wind brought the sound of laughing children to his ears. *Kids. Of course it's kids.* He sprinted down to the river, ignoring the cuts he was sure to get on his bare feet, certain that he would come out of the trees and find a group of kids sitting around laughing.

The laughter grew louder. He was getting close. He reached the end of the trail where the forest gave way to the beach. The laughter stopped. The beach was empty. The only sound was the river gently flowing and an occasional wave crashing into a dock.

"I know you're out here!" *He didn't.*

"I know who you are!" *Not a clue.*

"You won't get away with this!" *What could he do to stop them?*

The laughter started again, but faintly. Mason was nowhere near them. He fell to his knees. The laughter faded away until all that remained was the sound of the river. Mason buried his face in his blood-covered hands.

A red tennis ball bounced out of the trees and came to a stop against the side of his leg. Mason did not notice. He stayed that way until the sun came up.

As the campground brightened with the sun, Mason trudged back up the hill to their campsite. Amber was loading up the car. Everything was packed up except for the tent. She couldn't bring herself to move Jacoby's body.

Mason tripped over something as he watched Amber trying to keep her mind occupied. He looked down to see what he had kicked.

"Amber," he yelled. "Amber, get down here. You need to see this."

He should not have, but he couldn't help feeling relieved. He had been right all along. It never should have gone this far—he was horrified by what had happened to Jacoby—but now Amber would *have to* see what was really going on.

"What is it?" Amber was panting, trying to catch her breath. Her eyes were bloodshot and swollen from crying all night. It did not look like she had gone back to sleep. Mason couldn't blame her. He hadn't either.

"Look." He pointed at the object he had tripped over. It was a young tree branch, about three inches around. Or, at least it had been before it was stripped of its bark and sharpened on both ends. One of the tips was covered in dried blood. Jacoby's blood.

"Do you still think it was all in my head?"

"All what?"

"The Farm, the ball, Jacoby. All of it. It's the same person doing all of it. It has to be."

"Mason, now's not the time. Can we just go home?"

Neither of them said a word while they wrapped Jacoby in the bloody sleeping bag and laid it on the back seat. They did not talk as Mason took the tent to the dumpster next to the outhouse. Not one word as they started to drive off before Mason jumped out of the car to get the blood-stained stick. No one said anything until they were halfway home.

"How?" Amber asked.

"What?"

"How do you know it's all the same person?"

"The laugh," Mason said.

60 YEARS AGO

Eliza Montgomery was a typical six year old girl. She played with dolls. She cooked with her mother while waiting for her father to get home from work. She read stories and pretended to be the princess of her very own kingdom. And she loved sports. She dreamt of one day being the first girl to play for the New York Yankees. She told people she would be willing to play shortstop, but she wanted to be the pitcher.

During the summer before her sixth birthday, she was listening to a game on the radio with her dad. The Yankees were up by one against the Red Sox. It was the bottom of the ninth and there was a pitching change.

"The Yankees have made a call to their bullpen," the announcer said. The broadcast cut to a commercial as the closer walked out to the mound.

"That is going to be me someday," Eliza told her dad.

"Sure it is, honey, if that is what you want to do." Her dad sounded supportive but he was holding back laughter. He never told Eliza what he really thought about her dream. He didn't have to. When her birthday came around, all she wanted was a baseball so she could practice. He gave her a pack of red tennis balls instead.

She thanked him, but her face was unable to hide her disappointment. She was not going to let that stop her though. She would still practice as often as she could. She took those red balls with her everywhere she went.

8

Six weeks had passed since their camping trip and things had gotten worse for Mason. He had not slept more than four hours a night in over a month. He saw that little girl with the holes in her head every time he closed his eyes. And the ball. That red tennis ball followed him around the same way Jacoby used to when he was a puppy. He went to work. It was there. At home, it was there. In the bathroom, it rolled around in the sink while he washed his hands.

Mason and Amber had been talking about his dreams—and the ball—a lot. Amber started asking about it when his eyes began to look like they were sinking back into his head. He looked like a junkie. At first, Amber was worried that he might have started shooting up after the camping trip but Uncle Jim drug tested all of his employees every three weeks. If Mason had been using something, she would have known.

Amber listened to Mason spout out conspiracy theories about someone stalking him and trying to make him think he was losing his mind.

First, he blamed Jeremy.

"I taught that little bastard everything he knows. He would still be vacuuming crumbs from between the seats in those cars for minimum wage instead of selling them if I hadn't put in a good word with Jim. Now he's making six figures. Easy. But is that enough? He knows he'll never beat me, so he's trying to take me out of the game."

Amber reminded Mason that this all started before he went back to work at the car lot so it wouldn't make sense for it to be Jeremy.

"Okay, okay. But it started when I surprised you with that date at the Farm, right? What about that kid you tutored in high school? What was his name? Daryl... David... Devin? Devin! That guy was obsessed with you. Of course. It has to be him. He wants to get me out of the way."

"Mason, that is ridiculous. Devin asked me out one time, eight years ago. Before he knew we were dating. I haven't even heard from him since high school. You sound crazy."

"Crazy? I'm crazy?" Mason yelled. "Maybe I am crazy. This is all in my head. Is that what you want to hear? What about Jacoby? Oh, that's right, how could I forget? I carved a spear after you fell asleep. Then I stabbed our dog with it, took it out of the tent, and hid it by the river. Then I crawled back into my sleeping bag and tucked myself in under his dead body. That's exactly what happened. You caught me."

Amber's eyes became faucets. She slapped Mason across the face.

"I don't think you are crazy. But you need to realize that no one is stalking you. It's not a person doing this, but I don't think it's all in your head either."

Mason did not say anything. He put his hand on his cheek. The skin was raw and hot and had a perfect red outline of her hand on it. He nodded for her to continue.

"There's someone I think you should meet," Amber said.

***

"I don't know about this," Mason said.

They were standing on the sidewalk in front of a rundown building that was little more than a shack wedged between a Starbucks and a real estate office. A hand carved sign over the door read *Madame Ethelinda's Magick Shoppe*.

A bell chimed as Amber opened the door and pushed Mason into the building. Somehow, the beads hanging down from the windows managed to keep out all of the natural sunlight. The room was filled with an orange-yellow glow from the lamp next to the cash register. Incense burned in all four corners and on either side of the door. The haze of smoke stung Mason's eyes. Sitar music played softly from an iPod plugged in below the lamp.

As Mason's eyes adjusted to the dim light and clouds of smoke, a woman came out of the back room. Her hair was either streaked with gray or dirty blonde. It was impossible to tell in that light. Her shoulders rolled forward as she approached them. Even though her posture was terrible—she looked slightly hunchbacked—and she walked with a limp on her right side, her presence in the room was immense.

Madame Ethelinda approached Amber and gave her a hug, accompanied by a yellow smile. She was less enthusiastic with Mason. Instead of a hug, she gave him a quarter-bow with a little flourish of her hand. The smile remained but it was much less genuine. Mason did not mind one bit. He was still unsure what to make of all of this. A month ago, all he wanted was for Amber to believe him. Now that she did—and was actively trying to help—part of him wished that she still had her doubts. Something about that woman made his skin itch. She looked exactly the way he imagined the gypsy his mom had always threatened to sell him to would look.

"Come, sit. Sit," she said, primarily to Amber, with her thick Eastern European accent. They knew each other from a Facebook group for paranormal enthusiasts. That's what they called themselves. *Enthusiasts.* A bunch of headcases was what Mason thought of them as—at least he had, until all of this started.

She led them to a short, round table with no chairs in the back corner of the room. Madame Ethelinda took off her shoes before kneeling in front of the table. Amber did the same. Mason stood next to the four empty shoes. The two women stared at him. Neither said a word. They waited. Finally, Mason could not stand their silent gazes any longer and kicked off his own shoes. Amber smirked as Mason kneeled at the table next to her.

A tall candle stood at the center of the table. Madame Ethelinda lit it.

"Tell me," she said, again more to Amber than Mason, "what is it that you need from me?"

Amber looked at Mason. So did Madame Ethelinda. In the flickering candlelight, her eyes looked black. Her nose was long and crooked, like it had been broken and allowed to heal without being reset. *Throw in a couple of warts and paint her face green and she'd look just like a cartoon witch.*

"Go on, tell her," Amber said.

Mason looked at his girlfriend. This was her idea. *She* should be the one who had to tell the story. He was just along for the ride. Amber stared at him until he gave in again.

Mason recounted for Madame Ethelinda everything from the cemetery at the Farm, to the red ball showing up everywhere he went, and the girl in his dreams with the long teeth and holes in her head. "And then the same sick freak who is following me with the ball killed my dog."

"I see. I see." That's all she said.

Madame Ethelinda took the candle from the middle of the table and used it to light incense sticks that were evenly spaced around the outer edge of the table. She bowed her head and closed her eyes.

Mason looked at Amber. She shrugged and they sat in silence, waiting for Madame Ethelinda to say something. Mason tried to ask her if there was anything she could do. The gypsy woman held up a bony finger to silence him.

After three and a half minutes of silence, Madame Ethelinda raised her head.

"Join hands," she said. Amber took her hand and reached out for Mason's.

"Why?"

"Mason. This woman is trying to help you. Just do it, okay?" Amber said.

"So we are just supposed to believe that she can help when she's barely said two words the whole time we've been here? Why? Because she's in your online group of whack jobs. And she's what? Some kind of magic witch or something? No. No way. I'm out of here."

He pushed himself up from the table, but Madame Ethelinda slapped her hand down on top of his. Mason stopped. He made eye contact with her and the rest of the room seemed to fade out of focus. Her eyes were black and orange in the candlelight. Amber placed her hand on top of his other hand. A wave of warmth—and a little worry—washed over him and he dropped back to his knees.

The smell of incense was gone. So was the dim yellow light. The flame of the candle became the pale white of a full moon flickering on their faces. Madame Ethelinda's eyes changed again—not back to their normal blue-flecked green but to red.

A child's laugh filled the room. Mason was not the only one who heard it. Amber jumped at the sound. She tried to pull her hands back from the table. Mason grabbed her wrist and held tight. It was her idea and she had stopped him when he tried to leave. There was no way he was letting her get out of it now. No matter what happened next.

Madame Ethelinda smiled, red balls bounced where her pupils should have been. A sound, like the crash of a cymbal, rose up from between them. The candle had been knocked to the floor. The gold saucer that it had been sitting on slid across the table. It came to a rest just before falling off. In place of the candle at the center of the table was a mud-covered, red tennis ball.

Amber screamed and scrambled away from the table.

“We must keep our hands linked,” Madame Ethelinda said to Mason. He nodded and crawled over to Amber.

“Come on,” he whispered. “It’s just a ball.” He tried flashing her his salesman smile, but Amber just sat there, knees pulled up to her chest, rocking side-to-side as if to say *no* with her entire body.

Mason got behind her and slid his arms beneath her shoulders. He carried her back to the table and gave one of her hands to Madame Ethelinda.

“You’re all right.” He kissed her ear before taking her other hand and returning to his spot at the table. As the three of them rejoined their hands, the ball on the table started bouncing. The child’s laugh filled the room again.

Mason kept his smile on for Amber’s sake, but his whole body had broken out in gooseflesh and sweat began to run down the back of his neck. The ball kept bouncing. Higher and higher each time. Then it stopped. So did the laughter.

The silence seemed to be coming from a single spot in the room. Not possible, but somehow true. Madame Ethelinda looked up at the spot Mason was sensing.

Slowly, Mason turned his head to follow her gaze. Amber did the same. Madame Ethelinda was looking right at the girl from Mason’s nightmares.

“Oh my God,” Amber said.

“You can see her?” Mason should not have been surprised. She had seen the ball and heard the laugh, why wouldn’t she see the girl too? Part of him was relieved that she was finally experiencing what he had been dealing with. A separate part—smaller, but bigger than it should have been—was enjoying the fact that she could see something that supported her belief in the supernatural and was entirely unable to handle it.

"Welcome," Madame Ethelinda said.

The girl said nothing. Blood trickled down the sides of her face from the holes in her head. Her body had a magenta hue but it was muted. She seemed to be glowing gray. *"Her aura," Amber would say later.* After what felt to Mason like an eternity—a whopping thirty seconds or so—the girl moved toward the table. She was not walking exactly. Her legs seemed to be moving, but they were not touching the ground.

Mason's throat began to itch. He could not swallow. His shirt was glued to his back by a million beads of sweat and he was cold. So cold.

The girl stopped at the edge of the table. Her mouth fell open, revealing teeth that were too long and too sharp. Her laugh hit them as she grabbed her ball and it continued to bounce around the room as she dissolved. That was the only way Mason could describe it. She just kind of spread out in the air and disappeared. But she wasn't gone, of that Mason was sure. *Not gone. Everywhere.*

No one said anything for a long time. The orange-yellow glow of the lamp returned to the room. A streak of sunlight broke through the beaded curtain on the front window. That seemed to bring everyone back to the real world.

"Who was that?" Amber said under her breath, just in case the girl was still in the room with them.

"That's the girl of my dreams," Mason said. Amber didn't laugh.

"Congratulations," Madame Ethelinda said with a smile. Her teeth were more crooked than her nose and as yellow as the light from the lamp. "You have a ghost."

***

Amber let Mason drive them home. She sat in the passenger seat with her feet tucked up and her arms wrapped around her knees. Her eyes looked like they would fall out of her head if he hit a pothole. Mason tried to put a reassuring hand on her thigh as he drove, but she recoiled from his touch and turned to face out the side window.

When Mason pulled into the driveway, he got out and made it all the way to the porch before he realized that Amber was still sitting in the car. He went back and opened the door for her. She was rocking on the seat, muttering soundlessly to herself.

"Shouldn't I be the one freaking out?" he said, trying to lighten the mood. He unbuckled her seatbelt and pulled her to her feet. She did not fight him, but she was not helping either. Lifting her dead weight by one arm, he felt like he was going to dislocate his shoulder. He managed to get her to her feet, but he had to wrap his arms around her waist to keep her standing. That was when she started to resist.

"I'm the one being haunted, remember? Not you," Mason said as he pushed her toward the house. "Plus, you're the one who always believed in all this ghost stuff anyway. So help me out here."

At that, Amber snapped out of her shocked state and turned on him. She shoved him back toward the car.

"I *do* believe it. That's why my reaction is perfectly reasonable. Some little girl's spirit has latched onto you for God knows what reason. And she has been literally driving you crazy for months. And you're what? Totally cool with all of it now? No big deal, there's just this creepy little girl with *HOLES IN HER HEAD* haunting you. But it's all good. Is that it?"

"I never said that."

"You didn't have to," Amber said. "How do you see this all playing out?"

"I don't know. I know it's not real now. I don't have someone following me around trying to ruin my life. I guess I'll just ignore it until everything goes back to normal."

"You have got to be kidding."

The red ball bounced up to Mason's feet. He looked past Amber. Standing on the porch was the girl. There was no laughter this time. She looked confused. Maybe a little lonely, too.

"Nope," Mason said and smiled at Amber.

"You were just there with me, right? You saw all of that? I wasn't in that shop by myself?" Amber was yelling at this point. Mason looked around to see if any neighbors had made their way into their yards. A good lawn fight was better than cable in this neighborhood. No one was watching them. *Yet*. Except for the girl standing on the porch.

"I was," Mason said. He walked toward Amber, hoping she would start moving. She stood her ground. "Fine. The truth is that yeah, I was sorta freaked by the whole thing, but none of that was new for me. I'm glad to have an answer to what has been going on, if that really is the answer. But if it's not a real person, then I have nothing to worry about."

"She *was* a real person. And now she's haunting you. And you think you can just ignore her and she will go away? Ghosts don't just go away. If they could, they wouldn't be there in the first place. Don't you think we should figure out what she wants?"

"Don't need to. I can just tune it out now that I know it's not real."

"Mason! How can you still say it's not real?"

"Well..." He picked up the red ball that was still sitting at his feet. "Does this look real to you?" He tossed the ball up in the air a few times. All Amber could see was Mason holding his hand out and flicking his wrist up over and over.

"Exactly," he said. "You don't see it. And what about the porch? See anything there?"

"She's there?" Amber jumped behind Mason for cover. Mason looked at the figure on the porch and then took Amber by the shoulders.

"No one is standing on our porch. And I wasn't just tossing a ball. They aren't real. Nothing to worry about."

Mason led Amber by the shoulders to the front door. She dug her heels into the grass before stepping up onto the porch.

"Fine. I can go first. Will that make you feel better?"

Mason walked up to the door and put his key into the doorknob. The girl was inches from his arm as he turned it. He held his breath as he walked past her into the house. He had said all of the right things to get Amber to calm down, but he honestly did not know if he believed his own words anymore. The girl turned her head to watch Mason enter the house. He exhaled once he was inside the living room. When he turned around to face Amber, the girl was gone.

"Nothing to worry about," he said to Amber, unsure of which one of them he was trying to convince.

9

Amber sat at the dining room table while Mason cooked a quick spaghetti dinner. He said something from the kitchen but she was unable to hear it. The furnace kicked on and the air vent rattled. Amber leapt up and knocked over her chair. Mason heard the chair hit the floor and ran into the dining room. Amber had backed herself into the corner and was clinging to the wall.

"Are you okay? What happened?"

"I… I… I heard something. Is she here? She's here isn't she?"

Mason looked around the room. It was empty. And there was no one hiding in the shadows because there were no shadows. Amber had turned on every light in the house to make sure of that.

"It's just us," he said, not that he would have told her anything else even if the girl was there.

A hiss came from the kitchen. Amber jumped again.

"What was that?"

"The water is boiling over. That's all."

Mason went back to the stove to finish cooking. Amber followed. She stood behind him with her hands wrapped around his waist until the food was ready. She dug her fingernails into his hips every time she heard a creak or rustle. She had left her phone sitting on the table in the other room. It chimed to let her know that she had missed a call and she squeezed him hard enough to draw blood.

When the food was ready, Mason dished up a plate for each of them. He set the food on the table and picked Amber's chair up off of the floor. They both sat down at the table but Amber did not touch her food. Mason managed to take a few bites before Amber said something that made him lose what little appetite he had.

"You should eat," Mason told her.

"Not hungry." Amber's eyes were darting around the room, trying to make sure they were still alone.

"I really don't know why you are so worried. You heard what that psychic—or medium or whatever she is—said. That girl is the one who has been behind all of it. She's been here the whole time. You never saw her before and she never bothered you so you have nothing to worry about."

"What about Jacoby?" Amber said.

That was it. Mason dropped his fork and stopped chewing with a mouthful of spaghetti. He hadn't thought about that. If that creepy girl was responsible for everything since the asylum, then she had somehow managed to stab his dog. How could he ignore her and pretend that she couldn't do any real harm to him when she had killed Jacoby? And the ball? That certainly felt real when it hit him in the garage at work. It felt real in his hands when he picked it up. Even if no one else could see it. It *felt* real.

He covered his mouth with a napkin and filled it with half-chewed noodles.

"Let's go to bed," he said.

***

The next morning, Amber seemed a bit more like herself. She was out of bed before Mason and made eggs and bacon while he was in the shower.

She looked at something on her phone while Mason ate.

"You really should eat something," he said.

Amber grabbed a piece of bacon and bit off half of it without looking up from her phone. She kept scrolling as she chewed. She did put the phone in her pocket to walk him to the door, though.

"You're sure you don't need me to stay home?"

"I'm fine," she said. She kissed him on the cheek and gave him a gentle but firm push on the back to get him out the door. "Have a good day at work."

"Okay... I love you." Mason was not buying the total one-eighty that seemed to have happened overnight. He might have, but the purple-black circles under her eyes gave her away. He did not press her on it. When Amber wanted to talk about something she did. That was one of the things he loved about her. She never seemed to beat around the bush. It was a bit of a stretch, but he let himself hope that she might let the whole thing go and leave him to deal with it in his own way.

"Love you, too," she said. "I'm taking the day off work. Gonna do some research. I'll tell you what I find tonight."

Maybe not.

The sun was just beginning to rise as Mason left for work. He put his helmet on and rode off. He waved to Amber. She was still standing in the doorway but already had her phone up to her ear. He tried not to think about what she might make him try next. If it would help her cope with what Madame Ethelinda had shown them, then he would go along with whatever Amber wanted to do, but he would rather just ignore all of it and try to move on. He could deal with the sound of a ball bouncing along after him for the rest of his life, if it came to that. People live with tinnitus all the time. It would be just like that. He would get used to it. Eventually.

Mason turned off of their street. He was still thinking about Amber. Someone up ahead, on the other side of the street honked as a stoplight changed from red to green. He looked that way. There were two cars—the one that honked and one just starting to roll through the intersection. The light in front of Mason turned red. He slowed his bike to a stop and put his foot down on the pavement. He kept watching the other two cars. In another hour or so, there would be lines of traffic running in both directions, but no one else was on the road yet. As the second car made it through the intersection, it swerved into the center lane and the driver gave the finger to the first car as he raced past. Mason chuckled.

The exhaust squealed as the car sped away. Mason looked over to see if he could catch a glimpse of the other driver's reaction to being given the bird. Instead, his attention went to a figure standing on the corner caught his attention. It was the girl—*the ghost*—he was out of rational arguments to explain her being anything but.

The stoplight in front of Mason turned green. He was still focused on the ghost across the street. He started moving, still watching her as he passed through the intersection, turning his head as he rode down the street to keep his eyes on her. A car pulled to a stop at the intersection where she was standing and the headlights washed her out. Before Mason lost sight of the girl, he thought he had seen her starting to wave. For the rest of his commute, Mason had no trouble keeping his mind off of what Amber might have been doing at home.

He saw the girl three more times throughout the day. Once at the car lot in the bed of a truck, once in the showroom as he was waiting for a customer to finish filling out a credit application, and once in the mirror while he was washing his hands in the men's room. Each time, she had that damn red ball in her hands.

***

Amber had dinner on the table and was waiting in the doorway when Mason got home from work. The dark circles still surrounded her eyes but there was an excitement in them that Mason had not seen in years. She looked as giddy as she had when he picked her up in a limo for their high school prom.

"What's gotten into you?" he said, tucking his helmet under his arm.

"Oh nothing," she said. "I just took care of our little haunting problem."

"Is that right?"

"Come on, I'll show you." She grabbed his elbow and dragged him into the house. Amber high-stepped over the threshold of the door. "Watch your step."

Mason looked down. She had lined the doorway—along with the baseboards and window sills—with a thick band of salt. Mason followed her lead and tiptoed through the door. His nose began to itch as soon as he was inside. There was smoke drifting throughout the house and a pile of still-smoldering sage leaves on the coffee table.

"Looks like you really went all out today," Mason said.

"I did." Amber was bouncing with excitement. She had been preparing for something like this for as long as Mason had known her. Ever since meeting the ghost in her childhood home, she had watched and read everything she could find that was even remotely paranormal (she had even tried to start a club in high school, but the only other member was her cofounder). She lived her life in the spirit world—observing it, embracing it, communicating with it, and now protecting people from it. This was more like the reaction that Mason had been expecting after their trip to Madame Ethelinda's. She had not seen a ghost since Albert. Now that she had, she was pulling out all the stops.

They made their way into the dining room and sat down to eat.

"Did you see her today?"

"I did," Mason said. He considered lying to her, but took the change in her demeanor as a sign that she could handle the truth.

"What about now?"

"Not at the moment." Mason cut a piece off of his steak and put it into his mouth. Chewing, he hoped, would give him time to think of the right answer to whatever follow-up question she was about to ask. But she did not ask anything else.

"Good," she said. "But let me know if you do. I did enough cleansing today that she should be gone, but it's not all finished yet."

Mason laughed and started singing the *Ghostbusters* theme song like he had when they were running around the playground as kids.

Amber smiled. "Shut up and finish eating. I already did the floors, but I need your help to finish scrubbing the walls with lemon and cinnamon water."

After an hour, Amber dropped the rag she had been using to scrub the walls into a bowl of water.

"I think that should do it," she said. She carried the bowl back into the kitchen and dumped it into the sink. She flicked the switch for the disposal. Cinnamon sticks and lemon wedges were ground down to nothing and their scents filled the house.

"And if not, at least the house smells fantastic," Mason said as he tossed his rag onto the counter. He leaned down and kissed Amber. "Let's go to bed."

"Don't you want to wait and see if it worked?"

"If you think this will get rid of her, then it probably will. You're as close to an expert on this stuff as anyone."

"On what stuff?" Amber said.

"You know. Come on. Let's go."

"No I don't. What stuff?" Amber smiled.

"You're really going to make me say it?" Mason paused, sighed, then: "Ghosts, okay? You're a ghost expert. Now can we please just go to bed?"

Amber hooked his arm and skipped down the hallway. Seventeen years later, she had finally won the argument that had begun on the day they met.

***

Mason lay in bed staring up at the ceiling. Moonlight and shadows danced across his field of vision and the steady sound of a ball bouncing somewhere just outside the house beat like a metronome. It bothered him less than it had before. Like white noise, it was almost soothing. On the other hand, that girl. He would never get used to her. It wasn't necessarily fear—and not the holes in her head either—but *something*. Something about her was unsettling.

A cloud drifted in front of the moon and the bedroom filled with darkness. Mason closed his eyes. The last thing he thought about before falling asleep was what Amber had said before she went to sleep. *If you do see her again you can just ask her to leave. She might not even know that she's dead.*

10

His dream that night started the same as always. He was chasing his ball through the woods, never quite able to catch it. Then he came out onto the road and closed his eyes as the headlights bore down on him. The laughter grew louder. Almost unbearable. Then silence.

This time there was no whine, no pain in his temples. When he opened his eyes, he saw the girl. Blood dripped slowly from the holes in the sides of her head. She was laughing hysterically. Long gray teeth and greasy black hair dripped blood as well.

Mason blinked. The girl was gone.

He was standing in the middle of a cobblestone street. He looked around. It made him think of a Dickens book he had read years ago. Gas lanterns gave the street an orange glow. Snow was just beginning to fall. There were no lights in the windows of the buildings that lined the road. No cars anywhere—driving or parked. A train whistle blew somewhere in the distance. He pulled the sweater that he was now wearing tighter around his shoulders. He started walking, glancing back over his shoulder every few steps. He was alone, but it felt like someone was watching him. *Following* him.

He walked past three storefronts and stopped at the mouth of an alley just before the fourth. He turned around—all the way this time—to make sure that there was no one behind him. His eyes darted around the deserted street. When he felt convinced that he was alone, he turned down the alley. There were no lights. The moon was only a quarter full and not much light made it through the snow clouds. It was dark except for the lantern behind him and one at the far end of the alley. He bundled his sweater tighter and started to walk.

He could vaguely remember someone telling him that it wasn't safe to take the shortcut, but it would save him a full ten minutes of walking and the snow was coming faster by the second. The wind was picking up, too. As he left the circle of light from the streetlamp, the sense of being followed overwhelmed him. He looked back and saw nothing but the empty street that he had just left at the end of the empty alley. Still, he quickened his pace. He did not have far to go—something inside told him that if he could just reach the light of the street, he would be safe. He looked back again, and again he saw nothing. But the pit in his stomach grew tighter. He *knew* he was not alone.

He was carrying a bag. He did not know where it had come from or what was in it, but he dropped it and started to run. He had made it halfway down the alley. Too far to turn back now.

He heard a sound when the bag hit the ground that was much too loud to have been *just* the bag. And then he heard it again. And again. *Footsteps*. Someone was following him and no longer cared if they were found out. He tried to run faster, but the sound was getting closer and the light at the end of the alley seemed miles away.

The footsteps behind him rang in his ears, louder than his own. A gloved hand grabbed inside the collar of his sweater and spun him around. Mason was face-to-face with a large man—he looked to be at least twice Mason's size—wearing a rubber apron, thick rubber gloves, and goggles. He had a bag of his own strapped across his chest.

Mason stared at the reflection in the goggles. It was his reflection but he wasn't Mason. He was a much-too-thin woman with wavy red hair and large hoop earrings, wearing a white cardigan sweater on top of a short black dress. Mason wanted to scream. Or fight back against the giant that was holding him. He could do nothing but stare at the woman in the reflection.

The man threw Mason to the ground and held him there with one hand on his throat. He mounted Mason. Mason opened his mouth to scream, but the man pushed down harder on his neck so that nothing came out.

"Shh, shhh, shhhh," the man said as he unstrapped his bag.

Mason's legs flailed around, but the weight of the man sitting on his thighs was too much for him to buck off. The man opened his bag on the ground next to Mason's head.

Mason could not see everything that was in the bag but he saw what his attacker took out of it. The large man raised Mason's chin until his head was looking at the streetlamp that would have saved him if only he had been faster. He should have never taken the shortcut. Ten fewer minutes of cold was not worth his life.

The man was holding a scalpel. He ran the side of its cold steel blade down Mason's neck. As he continued to slide the blade down, he flicked his wrist and sliced each button off of Mason's sweater. Then he brought the scalpel back up to Mason's chest and cut open his shirt, or dress, or whatever it was that Mason was wearing. The night air on Mason's bare chest and abdomen was freezing but the steel of the blade was colder—the kind of cold that felt hot. Mason recoiled as the man moved the blade along his sternum.

"Shh, shhh, shhhh," the man repeated, even though Mason had given up trying to yell. In fact, he was holding his breath.

The man squeezed Mason's chest and sucked in a breath between clenched teeth. It sounded like the hiss of a snake. He shook his head and slapped Mason.

"Whore."

The large hand on Mason's throat pushed hard enough that he could not scream or say anything, but not so hard that it would keep him from breathing.

The man wanted to make sure that Mason—*the woman?*—knew exactly what was happening. He circled Mason's belly button with the tip of the scalpel. He leapt into a squat and used his shins to pin Mason's legs down instead of his knees, moved his hand from Mason's neck to mouth, and sliced. All in one synchronized moment. Mason screamed into the man's rubber palm. Tears welled up in his eyes, blurring his view of the man who was murdering him.

And then there was nothing. The pain was gone. So was the taste of rubber and the weight on his thighs.

The cold darkness of the alley was replaced by streaks of moonlight stretched across the ceiling and Amber's gentle snoring next to him.

Mason was able to catch the scream in his throat once he realized that he was in his own bed. His heart was pounding so hard that it felt as if his eyes would shoot out of their sockets if he kept them open but he could not bring himself to close them again. *Not yet.*

He lay there for a while—maybe minutes, maybe an hour—watching the shadows of the tree branches swaying on the ceiling. From the look of them, the wind was strong but he could not hear it. All he could hear was his heartbeat. Eventually, his heart slowed down. It helped when Amber rolled over and threw her arm across his chest. As his heartbeat returned to a normal pace, the sound of it was replaced by the ball. Mason grabbed Amber's hand as he rolled onto his side so that it did not move off of him. He pulled the blanket up to his chin and drifted back to sleep.

Once again, Mason found himself running through the trees chasing the bouncing ball. When the headlights approached, he closed his eyes. When he opened them, he was walking down an aisle of boxes and crates. Several tubs of ice lined the wall to his right. He was carrying a wire basket filled with crackers and fruit. Without thinking, he bent down and grabbed a bottle of Coca-Cola out of the ice. Reflected in the brushed metal of the ice bin, he saw himself and, once again, he was in a body that he did not recognize. The face looking back at him was round and bloated. He had hair—not much, but some—and thick glasses that sat crookedly on his nose.

He was wearing a sport coat and a dress shirt with buttons stretched to their limit.

Three men wearing black coats and fedoras entered the store waving weapons around—two pistols, one knife. The man with the knife pointed the tip at a man behind the counter. The two with pistols looked around the store for any movement. Mason crouched behind a crate. He pushed his bifocals up the bridge of his nose.

The men with the weapons were yelling at the man behind the counter about money. They were robbing the store. Mason started hyperventilating. He could not breathe. He patted the pockets of his slacks looking for something. They were empty. He put a hand over his heart like he hoped that holding it would slow its pace. There was a lump in the jacket pocket on his chest. He reached inside and pulled out an inhaler. Mason had never seen a dry powder inhaler in his life but he knew exactly how to use it. As soon as the powder hit his lungs, his heart began to slow down. He tried to hold it in for ten seconds like he was supposed to, but after about seven, the powder in his lungs made him cough.

The two men with guns turned toward Mason and started firing. One of the bullets hit him in the leg, just above the knee. Another took off half of his left ear.

The two men who had shot him stood over him. Mason was bleeding steadily from the ear and leg. They pointed their guns at him, ready to shoot him again. Mason's chest cinched around his lungs, refusing to let any air into them.

Mason turned his head to the right. The inhaler was on the floor, inches from one of the men's wingtip shoes. He stretched his arm toward it and wiggled his fingers. He could touch the inhaler, barely, but could not grab it. He tried again. His fingertip pushed the inhaler farther out of his reach. It slid up against the man's shoe.

"Check it out," the man said to his partner. "Fatso can't breathe without his medicine."

"A-a-asthma," Mason stammered. His face was as red as the label on the Coke bottle in his basket.

"Asthma? Ain't that one of those psycho things?"

"Psychosomatic," the second man said. "That's what the doctors call it. My cousin had it. They said his head wouldn't let him breathe seeing as how he missed his dead momma."

"So fatso wants his mommy?" the first man said as he kicked the inhaler down the aisle.

Mason's face turned from bright red to purple.

"I don't think we even need to shoot him," the first man continued. "Look at him. He's gonna fixate himself just sittin' there."

"Asphyxiate," the second man said.

"Huh?"

"It's asphyxiate, not fixate, you moron. But you're right. He won't make it much longer."

The second man walked back up to the counter to help the man with the knife get the money into a bag. The first man stayed. He waved his gun around in front of Mason's face, tapped him on the forehead with it, and laughed.

“Come on, fatso,” he said. “What’s the matter? You too fat to breathe? Or just too psycho?” He laughed again and stomped his size nine wingtip onto Mason’s stomach.

The pressure on Mason’s lungs got even tighter. His face began to change from purple to blue. His eyes bulged behind his glasses. A blood vessel in one of his eyes burst and turned the white to red. The man standing over him laughed again. It was a high-pitched, machine gun–sounding laugh. The man dug his heel harder into Mason’s stomach.

The pain from the bullet wound in his leg and his missing ear faded. It was replaced by the pressure building behind his eyes. Mason’s arms and legs began to spasm. The man continued pushing down on Mason’s stomach. The edges of Mason’s vision turned black and then the man was gone.

Mason shot upright in his bed. He gasped for air—loud enough that he woke Amber. He was panting, over and over, trying to make up for all of the breaths he had been unable to take in his dream.

Amber sat up next to him and put her hand on the back of his neck. Mason jumped away from her and fell to the floor. He tucked his head and curled himself into a ball.

“Mason, what’s wrong? What happened?”

Mason said nothing, just continued to gasp for air.

Amber slid down to the floor. She placed his head in her lap and wrapped a blanket around him. They sat that way for six hours until the sun rose.

***

Amber was still asleep on the floor when Mason went to the bathroom. He had not gone back to sleep. The dreams felt too real. He checked his ear in the mirror to make sure it was all there. It was. He looked for bruises on his neck or cuts on his stomach. Nothing. There was no bullet hole in his leg. But he *had* felt all of it.

Mason splashed some cold water from the sink on his face and stared at himself in the mirror. It was his reflection. Not the skinny, redheaded woman or overweight man with glasses. And he wasn't hurt. Not physically at least. That was something. He splashed more water on his face and then got in the shower.

When he got out, he went to the closet. He started putting on his suit to go to work. He had his shirt buttoned and tucked in and was fiddling with his tie—he always had trouble with the knots—when Amber walked up to him and ripped the tie out of his collar.

"What do you think you are doing?"

"I *was* getting dressed for work."

"*Nuh-uh*. I already called Uncle Jim. You aren't going anywhere until we figure this out."

"Figure what out?" Mason said.

"Figure what out?" Amber repeated. "You had a full-blown breakdown last night. We had to sleep on the floor! And you couldn't even tell me what was happening."

"To be fair, you slept on the floor. I was just lying on it. And I didn't ask you to get down there with me."

"You didn't have to. You looked like death." Amber paused and looked Mason up and down. "You still do. I'm not letting you out of this house until you tell me what is going on so we can fix it." She took Mason's arm and pulled him to the bed. She made him sit down and handed him a cup of coffee.

Reluctantly, Mason took a sip and recounted both of his nightmares for Amber, sparing no detail.

"But it was just a dream," Mason said. He took another sip of coffee.

"No," Amber said. "That was no normal dream. We have a lot more work to do."

***

Amber put on a pot of coffee for Mason and sat him down at the dining room table. She grabbed a blanket from the back of the couch and draped it around his shoulders. When the coffee finished brewing, she poured him another cup and kissed the top of his head. Mason's hair was still damp from the shower. She wiped the excess water from her lips.

"Don't move," she told him. "I have to go double-check a few things. I'll be back soon."

And then Mason was alone. The house was quiet except for the wind blowing against the sliding glass door behind him.

A drop of coffee slid down the side of the carafe and sizzled out of existence on the hot plate underneath it. The sound of the coffee pot made Mason jump. His own coffee sloshed over the rim of his mug, burning his wrist. Mason set the cup down on the table and walked into the kitchen, blanket still draped over his shoulders. He turned on the tap and held his wrist under the cold water. He felt a ball roll up against the side of his foot but ignored it.

Mason turned off the water. His eyes drifted to the window above the sink as he dried his hands. Reflected in the pane of glass, he saw her. The girl.

(She might not even know that she's dead)

Mason turned around to face her. The holes on the sides of her head were oozing blood so dark that it looked black. He had not noticed before, but she was wearing what looked like a hospital gown.

He shrugged the blanket off of his shoulders and stood up as tall as he could. *Make yourself big,* he told himself. *It works with bears, why wouldn't it work with little girl ghosts?* He took a step toward the girl.

She smiled. Her mouth opened, revealing her long, sharp teeth. Her eyes widened with excitement. Mason froze. He took a deep breath and puffed out his chest.

"Leave me alone," he said. *Friendly but firm, that's what Amber had said.* The girl did nothing.

"Leave me alone," he repeated. "Get out of my house."

Still the girl did not react. Her gape-mouthed smile and wide eyes remained. Mason thought of Jacoby. It was the same look he used to always give when he was waiting for Mason to throw his ball or give him a treat—the perfect combination of excitement and anticipation. Mason halfway expected the girl to start barking at him.

The thought deflated Mason. He was tired. And scared. And tired of being scared. His shoulders slumped. All of the authority left his voice.

"Why are you doing this to me? Can't you go be dead somewhere else?"

The girl reacted that time. The smile fell from her face. Her eyes turned down to the floor. The girl still looked like the ghost that had been terrorizing Mason. But there was more to it than that. She was *also* a sad little girl standing in his kitchen, crying because he had asked her to leave.

"No, no, don't do that," Mason said. "You don't have to be sad." For a moment, Mason forgot about himself. He took a couple of steps toward her, thinking he could console her and make everything better.

"What am I doing?" He stopped. "Get out. Stop crying and go. You don't get to cry. You are the one ruining my life."

He rose back up, inflating himself as he approached her. The girl seemed to shrink. She squatted down and grabbed her knees. She buried her face into her lap and shook her head.

A smirk came over Mason's face as he towered over her. Amber had been onto something after all. He could feel it working.

"Wouldja lookit this arsehole," said a woman's voice behind Mason. Then louder, and slower: "Just throw her the bloody ball, ya twit."

"L-l-leave him alone. He can't hear you a-anyway," a man's voice—nasally and wheezy—responded.

"Oh I'm sorry. Would it be better if I st-st-stuttered?"

Mason turned around. The two figures—a man and a woman—stood just outside the kitchen. They were the reflections he had seen in his dream. A scrawny redheaded woman and a short, round man. The woman was wearing a white cardigan with a dark red stain over her stomach. The man was missing part of an ear and had a hole in his pants just above his right knee. Neither of them had that gray glow like the girl did—the woman glowed a pinkish red and the man, a light brown.

"Sh-shut up Gertrude. You kn-know I can't h-h-help it."

"Don't you call me that," the woman said. "My name is Ruby."

"*Was.* That was your wh-whore name. You're not a whore anymore. Even if you could be, I'm the only one who can see you and..." The man paused. He looked her over and waved an arm at her. "N-n-no thank you."

"What the hell is happening?" Mason asked. The question was rhetorical but Gertrude/Ruby answered him anyway.

"That little girl just wants to have a catch and you're being a right wanker about it."

Mason walked between the two newcomers. He stared down at his feet and shook his head as he walked into the other room.

"That's it. I really am losing my mind," he muttered to himself as he paced around the living room.

"Not crazy, love," the woman said, following him. "You can see us now is all. We've always been here."

"N-n-not always," the fat man said. He was following Mason too, but he had a heavy limp and had not made it out of the dining room. He stopped to lean against the table. He took an inhaler—the same one Mason had used in his dream—out of his jacket pocket and put it up to his lips. The inhaler had the same tan glow that he had.

"Long enough," the woman said. "And what are you using that thing for? You're dead. You don't have to breathe anymore. What good is lung medicine gonna do ya?"

Mason stopped pacing.

"You already know you're dead? So telling you won't get you to leave me alone?"

"Of course we know we are dead. Just lookit us. This sweater used to be white. Do ya think I'd be caught dead wearing it with such a stain if I weren't already dead? And what about Tubs over there? Well... nevermind. He didn't have much to work with anyway."

"Tubs?" Mason looked at the man.

"The name's T-T-Timmy," the fat ghost said between gasps. He was still trying to catch a breath that he apparently did not need. Mason nodded.

"And you're... Gertrude?" Mason said to the woman. Timmy laughed himself into needing another puff of his inhaler. Maybe it was a comfort thing, something from his life that he wouldn't—or couldn't—leave behind.

"Shut it," she snapped at Timmy. "Ruby," she said to Mason.

"Okay," Mason said without allowing himself time to think about how crazy he must be to think he was *actually* having a conversation with two ghosts in his living room while a third was crying in the kitchen. "So you guys know you're ghosts. What about her?"

He pointed toward the kitchen. "Will she leave me alone if I tell her that she's dead?"

"You leave that poor girl alone," Ruby said.

"Poor girl? She's doing this to me! She needs to leave me alone. I'm not doing anything."

"Maybe that's your problem," Ruby said. "She just wants you to play with her."

"*She's* my problem," Mason yelled.

Timmy had finally made his way into the living room, but before he had a chance to contribute anything to the conversation, the front door swung open.

"Who are you talking to?" Amber asked.

Mason turned to face her. Then looked over his shoulder, first at Ruby, then Timmy. He turned back to Amber.

"Is she here?" Amber said. "She got into the house? Did you try telling her to leave?"

Mason looked at Ruby again. She gestured toward Amber. *Go ahead.*

"It didn't work," Mason said. Not entirely a lie, but he left out the fact that it was working until he was interrupted by two new ghosts. That was something he was going to keep to himself.

Amber did not say anything but the look on her face told Mason more than enough. She was disappointed in herself for not getting rid of his ghost. She had been so sure that she did everything right.

Amber went straight to the bedroom. Mason followed her. She sat down on the foot of the bed and flipped open her laptop.

"Just give me five minutes," Amber said when she saw him watching her from the doorway. Mason shrugged and turned to walk back down the hallway. "Close the door for me, would you?" He did.

Back in the living room, Ruby and Timmy were still standing—*do ghosts stand?*—by the coffee table. Ruby was flicking Timmy's half-gone ear.

"Kn-kn-knock it off," Timmy said, trying to shoo her hand away from his head like a fly.

"So, what? You guys are just always going to be around now?" Mason asked.

"We were here b-before. You just c-couldn't see us," Timmy said.

"That would be a *yes*, if you couldn't tell," Ruby said. She landed one last flick on Timmy's ear and then turned her attention toward Mason.

"Why?" he said. "Couldn't you find something better to be doing?"

"Trust me, love, if I could I would. It's something about the way we died that keeps us here."

"Yeah," said Timmy, "d-d-do you th-think I wanted to get shot t-t-twice and then suffocate to death? Or that sh-she wanted to get sl-sliced up in an alley?"

"He's right. It certainly was not the most pleasant way to go."

"I would've loved to see it , though," Timmy said. Ruby turned and punched him in the gut. He let out a comic-sounding "oof" and started coughing.

"Wait," Mason said, "that actually happened? Those messed up dreams were real?"

"That's right. You saw our last living memories through our own eyes. Probably, whatever opened you up to that little girl opened you to us as well. Which would explain why you can see us now," Ruby said.

"But why me?" Mason asked.

Before Ruby could say anything else Amber came out of the bedroom. She had heard Mason's question and thought he was talking to himself. *Having a little pity party, her mother would have said.* She set the computer down on the edge of the couch and wrapped him in a hug.

"It's going to be okay," she said. "We will figure this out. Together."

11

Mason decided not to tell Amber about the new ghosts. She already blamed herself for the girl. She had not been able to get rid of her despite trying everything she knew about exercising ghosts. He was not going to add two more to her plate when she was already struggling with the one she knew about.

That was a month ago.

Mason went back to work the day after he met Ruby and Timmy. He was not mentally ready, but he knew how to fake it. For the most part, things were normal. The girl with the ball had not shown herself since he made her cry in the kitchen. As for Ruby and Timmy, they were around—like they said they would be—but they stayed on the periphery. Mostly, they just pestered each other. It was like watching a prepubescent sibling rivalry. Mason found it almost amusing. And, more importantly, he got used to it.

***

Every Monday morning, Jim made the entire sales team show up an hour early. He called it professional development. Really it was a weekly reminder of which cars had been on the lot for too long. It was also when he announced the salesman of the week.

He always started with the salesman who had the lowest numbers and worked his way up. It made it more dramatic that way. Though, how dramatic it could really be was up for debate. Jeremy always won.

Mason tuned it out. Instead, he turned to watch the drama unfolding next to him. Ruby had just said something to Timmy that made him start hyperventilating. As he reached for his inhaler, Ruby swatted it out of his hand and sent it flying across the room. Mason laughed to himself. Ruby immediately turned her attention to him.

"Something funny, love?"

"No, I... no," Mason said.

"Bloody hell. Don't tell me that I am going to have to put up with another stammering imbecile."

"Don't worry about me," Mason said, still with a chuckle in his throat. "I'm just enjoying the show."

As Mason said that, Jim announced the third place salesman. Out of habit, Jeremy stood up from his front row seat, getting ready to shake Jim's hand when he was named the winner. Then he would give his own brief pep talk to the staff like he had every Monday for nearly two years. He had been the top salesman every week since Mason had quit the first time he worked at the lot.

"Second place this week goes to Jeremy which means our salesman of the week is Mason Turlock," Jim said.

Jeremy paused halfway between his chair and Jim. He looked back at Mason, laughing in the back row. Jeremy rushed up to Jim.

"You've got to be kidding. *He* beat me?" Jeremy whispered.

"Mason's good," Jim said. "One of the best who ever worked for me. But you should know that. He trained you didn't he? You shouldn't be surprised."

"Yeah, maybe. But seriously? He's not even paying attention. Look at him. He's sitting back there talking to himself. The guy is batshit."

"Don't know what to tell you kid. Numbers don't lie," Jim said. Then he turned back to the rest of the staff. "Okay, meeting's over. Let's get to work and see who is gonna come out on top this week."

The sales team started filing out of the meeting room past Mason. He stood up and waited for them to clear out. The last in line was Jeremy, who checked Mason with his shoulder on his way by. Mason stumbled back into his chair and had to sit on it to keep from falling. Ruby laughed. Mason looked at her and furrowed his brow.

"What?" she said. "I'm just enjoying the show."

Jim was right behind Jeremy. He reached out a hand to help Mason up from the chair.

"Don't worry about Jeremy. He's a bit salty now, but he'll get over it. Just isn't used to coming in second. He'll have to get used to it again now that you're back though, won't he?"

"I guess so," Mason said, only then realizing that he had been the top salesman. Mason started toward the door.

"Give me a hand with these chairs, would ya?" Jim said. "It'll give Jeremy a headstart so he won't have any excuses when you beat him again this week."

"Sure thing, boss."

Mason started folding up the chairs and stacking them on the cart parked against the back wall. He had finished two rows when Jim cleared his throat. Mason stopped.

"So," Jim said. "You know I love you and Amber like my own. And she says everything is fine. Whatever it is you had going on is good now. I want to take her at her word. You're here, performing, and numbers don't lie. But I gotta ask."

"Ask what?" Mason said.

"Something still ain't right. Something she doesn't wanna tell me. But something ain't right. Right? I mean for God's sake, you're sitting back here talking to yourself all morning."

Ruby howled with laughter. Timmy nodded. They were standing just behind Jim. Together, the three of them almost looked like those cartoons where a guy has an angel on one shoulder and a devil on the other. It wasn't hard for Mason to figure out which one was which.

"J-J-Just tell him the t-t-truth," Timmy said.

Mason ignored him.

"I'm fine. Just a little stress. Nothing to worry about. Really."

Mason returned to the chairs. Jim watched him for a moment, studied him. Something was off, that much was certain. But Jim could not put his finger on what it was and if Mason didn't want to tell him then he'd leave it alone. *For now.* If it started affecting his sales, though, then all bets would be off.

Jim watched Mason clean up the meeting room for another minute before going back to his office. Once the door swung shut, Mason turned to Timmy.

"What the hell was that, Timmy? You think I should go around telling everyone I can see dead people? They'd lock me up for sure."

Ruby was still laughing.

"And you," Mason pointed at her. "I know you supposedly don't have a choice of where to be now that you're a ghost—which makes no sense at all by the way—but would you mind keeping it down? I can't pretend you don't exist when all I can hear is your incessant cackling."

"Best be watching your tone, love. You're stuck with me like it or not. And you might not like me when I'm angry."

"Oh yeah? What are you like the Incredible Hulk or something?"

"I-incredible what?" Timmy asked.

"Nevermind. Just go back to bugging each other and leave me alone," Mason said. He put the last of the chairs on the cart and pushed it into the storage closet.

Mason shut off the light in the closet and turned to leave. He was ready to get out on the lot to try doing something that would keep his mind busy. When he turned around, the girl was standing in the doorway, kicking her toe into the floor, like a pitcher on the mound, and bouncing her ball.

She was not smiling this time, not trying to get Mason to play with her. Ruby saw the look on Mason's face and looked over at the doorway. When she saw the girl, she fell into another fit of laughter.

12

Mason made it through most of the rest of the day without getting stuck in anymore conversations with the ghosts. But they were there. All three of them—sometimes all together, sometimes by themselves—were always in sight. It was like watching a movie with the volume muted. And the girl still was not smiling. Her razor-sharp teeth were not something Mason thought he would miss, but her blank, joyless stare was worse. Much worse. It made his entire body itch.

As he rode home that evening, Mason thought about his last customers of the day. A young couple—older than Mason and Amber but not by much—had bought a gently-used, certified pre-owned, 2015 Ford Focus.

"She's pregnant," the man had said. He had dirty blonde hair that hung down to his shoulders and smelled vaguely of weed—it was not a fresh smell, more like he had smoked a few days before and forgot to wash his shirt. "We need something a bit safer."

The man handed Mason the keys to a 1982 Volkswagen Vanagon. The paint was chipped and faded orange. The seats needed to be reupholstered—they had the same stale pot smell as the man and the cloth had several small tears. But it had all original parts and only 110,000 miles on the odometer.

"I know it needs some *TLC,* but it's a classic," the man continued. "I want to make sure we are getting a fair shake on the trade-in before we sign anything."

Mason had played this game before, but the guy had a point. WIth a little bit of work, Jim would be able to flip it for a huge profit.

"Let me see what I can do," Mason said while showing off his trademark smile. He gave the couple some paperwork to fill out and went back to the "office" to check with his "supervisor." The office was really the break room and his supervisor was a can of Dr. Pepper from the vending machine. He sipped from the can and scrolled through a few articles on his phone.

"You're n-n-not a v-v-very good p-person are you?" Timmy asked. Mason coughed and tried—unsuccessfully—not to spray all twenty-three flavors across the table.

Mason said nothing, as he took a paper towel from above the sink and wiped up the soda. He took a deep breath, put on his salesman smile, and went back into the showroom to the table where his customers were waiting.

"Good news," Mason said as he sat down across from them.

"I sure hope so," the woman said. "We've been sitting here for twenty minutes."

Mason smiled at her and wrote something on the back of one of the forms.

"I think you'll agree that this was worth the wait."

He slid the paper across the table. Mason pointed to the three numbers he had written: the trade-in amount, total purchase price, and monthly payment.

"Can you give us a couple of minutes to talk it over?" the man asked.

"Of course," Mason said, still smiling. "Take your time." He went back to the break room to finish his soda.

When he opened the door, he saw Timmy still standing there.

"What now?" Mason said.

"W-w-why are you l-l-lying to that nice c-couple?"

"I'm not lying. I'm doing my job?"

"What's all this about, then?" Ruby asked. Mason was not sure where she came from. He had not seen her when he first entered the room.

"Nothing," Mason said. He picked up his half-full can of Dr. Pepper and threw it in the garbage.

"He's lying t-to those nice f-f-folks out there," Timmy told Ruby.

"Is that so? Good for you, love."

"I'm not," Mason said to Timmy. "I'm not," to Ruby.

"There's no shame in it. Gotta look out for yourself," Ruby said. Again, Mason imagined them as a cartoon angel and devil. He fought the urge to laugh.

"Just stay out of my life," Mason said and went back to his customers. "Well, have we come to a decision?" he said when he reached their table.

"We'll take it," the woman said, somewhat reluctantly.

"That's great," Mason said. He pulled another stack of paperwork out of the folder sitting on the table.

"See?" Timmy said to Ruby. They had followed Mason from the breakroom. "T-t-terrible p-person."

Mason's eyes darted over to Timmy as he slid the papers across the table to the couple.

"Just a few more signatures and I can get you the keys to your new car."

"Hold on," the woman said, placing her hand on the stack of papers. "What was that look?"

"Always look them in the eye." That's what he had told Jeremy. "Otherwise they will think you're up to something." It was rule number one. And he broke it.

"What look?" Mason said. The couple looked at each other. The woman pushed the paperwork back toward Mason.

"We want another fifteen hundred on the trade," she said.

Ruby started laughing. She really did seem to enjoy messing with Mason's life.

"I don't think I can do that," Mason said.

"Th-there he goes. L-l-lying again."

"We're leaving," the woman said to her husband. They pushed their chairs back and stood up. The couple walked past Mason. He was willing to let them leave if it meant Timmy and Ruby would leave him alone, until he saw Jeremy on the other side of the showroom. He was shaking hands with an older man and handing him a set of keys. Jim was standing in his office doorway. He gave Jeremy a thumbs up. Jeremy nodded in acknowledgement and Jim pointed at the couple about to leave the showroom—Mason's customers. Jeremy ran through his usual congratulations and see-you-next-time routine with the old man and started jogging across the showroom toward Mason's customers.

Mason kicked his chair back and turned around.

"Wait." The couple looked at Mason. Jeremy continued toward them but slowed to a walk. "I can get you another two thousand."

The woman smiled at her husband and walked back to the table. Timmy watched over their shoulders as they signed the papers. He nodded at Mason.

"W-w-well d-done."

Mason felt a smile stretch across his face, almost like he was proud to have earned the overweight ghost's approval. Or maybe he was happy about helping this couple get a better deal than they should have for their new family. Either way, it felt good.

With the paperwork finished, Mason stood up to shake hands with his customers and give them the keys to their new car. Jim was standing behind him. He put his hand on Mason's shoulder during the handshake and grabbed the keys off of the table before Mason could reach them.

"Congratulations folks. I'm sure you're going to love your new car. But, if you ever stop loving it, make sure you bring it back and we will find you another one to love," Jim said as he handed the keys across the table. He smiled and waved at them and squeezed Mason's shoulder as the couple left the showroom. He stayed like that until the door had closed behind the couple. "A quick word, Mason?"

Jim led Mason into his office.

"Close the door and have a seat."

The conversation with Jim was short and pretty much exactly what Mason had expected. He had overpaid for a trade-in and was cutting into Jim's bottom line. To make up for it, Mason was going to have to do all of the work to get the van ready for the lot—mechanical, paint, detailing—and he was going to do it during his time off for no pay.

"Or," Jim said, "I can keep the commission from the Focus you just sold them."

"I'll do it," Mason said.

Mason got up and opened the door. The girl was standing just on the other side of it, her eyes wide and unblinking. The holes in her temples were oozing. She bounced the ball. It made a heavy, wet sound on the tile floor before returning to her gray hand. Her overgrown fingernails—filed into daggers—wrapped around the ball. Slowly, her lips curled up into a smile, revealing her long gray teeth. Mason slammed the door closed and pressed his back against it.

Jim yelled at Mason to get out of his office. Mason held his breath and turned the doorknob with his eyes closed. When he opened them he saw only the showroom. He exhaled heavily and decided to call it a day.

***

"She's back," Mason told Amber as they were getting into bed. He filled her in on everything that had happened that day—except the conversations with Timmy and Ruby, of course. Amber still did not know about them.

She immediately placed a call. When she hung up the phone she looked at Mason.

"We are going back to see Madame Ethelinda in the morning. She is going to do whatever it takes to get rid of this girl for good."

***

When they got to Madame Ethelinda's shop, it had a much different feel than the first time they had been there. The sun had not come up yet. There was no light dancing through the beads on the windows. They were not met at the door with a smile and hug, but with the face of a tired old woman. Except her eyes. They were not tired. They were sharp and focused. Determined. Confident. They were the eyes of a much younger woman.

Madame Ethelinda locked the door after Mason and Amber were inside. She led them across the shop to a door with a sign hanging on it. The sign was a stick figure person inside a circle covered with a big red *X*. Scrawled across the bottom were two words. *Keep Out*. Madame Ethelinda opened the door and ushered them through.

A single lightbulb hung from a chain in the center of the ceiling. The room had a white tile floor surrounded by four plain white walls. There were no windows. It was empty, save for a single three-drawer filing cabinet and what used to be a massage table covered with a single white sheet. What the table was currently used for, Mason did not know, but he had a feeling that it was not anything quite as nice as a massage.

"On the table," Madame Ethelinda said. She went to the cabinet and rummaged around. Mason climbed onto the table. Just as he settled himself onto it, Madame Ethelinda turned around. Her hands were full of several small bags and bottles. She sighed. "Pants and shirt off first."

Amber laughed. She couldn't help it. Madame Ethelinda's head snapped in her direction.

"You. Not another sound or you leave," she said.

Amber pantomimed zipping her lips together and took Mason's shirt and pants from him as he got back onto the table.

Mason lay back, staring up at the lightbulb. Madame Ethelinda set her handful of supplies near his feet. Bottles clinked as she prepared for whatever she was about to do. Mason raised his head and tucked his chin to his chest, trying to see what she was doing. Madame Ethelinda—without looking—reached a hand up to his face and pushed his head back onto the table.

"No moving." She took the cork out of two of the bottles and poured their contents into a small saucer. She added some powder from one of the bags and stirred it all together with the long nail of her pinky finger. She dabbed her fingernail on her tongue and decided that the mixture was ready.

The old gypsy woman opened another bag—black velvet with a gold drawstring. She dumped out fifteen needles between Mason's feet. They were not rusted, but were no longer the silver color that they had once been. One needle was twice the size of the others.

Madame Ethelinda again told Mason not to move. She dipped each small needle into the saucer before sticking it into Mason. She started with his feet—one needle in the big toe of each foot. Then one on the inside of either thigh. One needle below the bottom rib on his left side. Same thing on the right. Each time the tip of a needle pierced his skin, Mason felt his muscle fibers grab the needle and hold it in place. One needle went on the outside of both hands and one on the inside of each elbow. Every needle caused a spasm that he was scolded for.

(no moving)

One on the top of each shoulder—both caused his arms to jerk and left him stuck in an extended shrug. Madame Ethelinda pushed his shoulders back into their normal position and continued.

"The potion draws the spirit to you and the needles pin it in place so that it cannot leave before we do what must be done," she said, responding to his involuntary shrug as if he had actually asked a question.

The final two small needles went into the tops of his ears. Madame Ethelinda rolled the big needle in the remaining solution. After the metal was thoroughly soaked, she stuck it in the bridge of his nose, directly between his eyes. She tapped on the back of it several times.

Mason could barely feel anything despite the size of the needle, but still he winced with each tap.

Madame Ethelinda leaned over and told him to close his eyes. He did, but then opened them immediately when he heard the click of a lighter. She was holding the flame to the needle between his eyes.

"Whoa! What are you doing?" Mason tried to lift his arm to push her away but the needles prevented his muscles from moving. Instead, a knot formed around each needle as his muscles clenched and tightened into rocks.

"Do not move. We have to draw the spirit to us. The flame is the way we activate the potion."

"Yeah, just relax Mason," Amber said, still smiling.

Before he could respond, the girl appeared at the end of the table. Mason couldn't see her, but he could hear her ball.

Madame Ethelinda kept the flame on the needle. The girl bounced the ball faster as the needle in Mason's face began to glow orange. With the agility of a much younger woman, Madame Ethelinda flicked the lighter closed and lunged to the end of the table. She snatched the ball away from the girl.

As soon as Madame Ethelinda's hands closed around the red tennis ball, she fell back onto the cold tile floor. Her eyes rolled up until all that remained visible were the whites. Amber shrieked.

"What? What's happening?" Mason asked. He could not raise his head from the table to see what was going on. His entire body felt like someone was rocking him back and forth, even though it did not move an inch. The lightbulb above his face seemed to start spinning on the end of the chain.

The lightbulb spun faster. Madame Ethelinda lay motionless on the floor. The girl let out a low noise that resembled the growl Jacoby used to let out whenever the Fedex truck stopped at their house.

Mason's stomach began to churn. And then everything stopped. The spinning light, the feeling of being rocked, the girl's guttural growling. All of it.

Madame Ethelinda's eyes returned to normal and she crawled to her feet. She left the ball on the floor.

"What's all this, then," said a British woman's voice. Apparently Ruby had joined the party, which meant Timmy was in the room as well.

"Great," Mason said under his breath.

"Her name is Eliza Montgomery," Madame Ethelinda said, pointing at the girl.

"W-w-we could h-have told you th-that."

"Okay," Amber said to Madame Ethelinda, "but who are they?"

"You can see them?" Mason said. Madame Ethelinda said nothing. She took the needle out of Mason's face and began removing the others.

"What are you doing?" Amber blurted out, ignoring Mason's question. "Won't that let them leave before we can get rid of them for good?"

"I can not help you," Madame Ethelinda said.

"Wait, what do you mean you could have told me?" Mason said to Timmy.

"You never asked," Timmy said.

"Why not?" Amber asked Madame Ethelinda.

"She's you," Madame Ethelinda and Ruby said to Mason at the same time.

"And I believe that they are too." Madame Ethelinda pointed at Ruby and Timmy. They were flanking the girl, Eliza.

"N-n-no kidding," Timmy said.

"Would you shut up?" Mason said.

"They are talking?" Amber asked.

"Yes. You don't hear them?"

"No."

"That'd be nice," Mason said.

"How are you so calm about this? You all of a sudden have two more ghosts following you around and you're just chatting with them like old friends?"

"That's right," Ruby said. "Just a few old mates having a bit of a chin-wag, aren't we?"

"Just shut up for a minute," Mason said.

"I'm just—" Amber started.

"No, not you. Her." Mason cocked his head toward the ghosts. Ruby nodded. "Thank you."

"These spirits are tethered to you because they *are* you," Madame Ethelinda said. "They are your past selves. Different personifications of the same soul."

"So I used to be a prostitute and a fat guy with asthma? And that creepy little girl?"

"Hey! Watch it!" Ruby said. Mason snapped his head around toward her. "Sorry."

"It's not quite as simple as that but yes. In a way. They are older incarnations of your spirit and as such cannot be removed by any exorcism or ritual. They are disturbed by something in their past and have reached out to the current embodiment of their soul for help."

"So that's your big reveal?" Mason said. "The creepy girl with holes in her head is disturbed? What a shocker."

Madame Ethelinda ignored Mason's interjection and continued. "They each have a reason for choosing to appear to you."

"Yeah. I know. They want to ruin my life," Mason said. Ruby blew him a kiss.

"Why would they do that, Mason?" Amber said. "If they are versions of you, then your life is their life." She looked at Madame Ethelinda. "Right?"

"Correct. I believe they need your help. Something is keeping them here with you. They may not even know what it is. That is why they need you."

"So I have to help them to get rid of them. Fine. But that girl... Eliza? She hasn't said one word in all this time. How am I supposed

to help her if she doesn't tell me anything about herself? All I know is her name."

"I have told you everything that I know," Madame Ethelinda said. "I can be of no more help to you."

60 YEARS AGO

From *The Herald*:

Eliza Montgomery had been missing for two weeks. She was last seen by her parents playing with a red ball near the forest on the edge of their property just after dusk. The other end of the forest borders Highway 63. A search party made up of friends and neighbors was formed when Eliza, age 6, did not come home for dinner. Though they did not find her, or her body, they began to fear the worst. The search continued in full force for three days. That is when people truly began to lose hope of ever finding Eliza.

By the end of the first week, the search party had only two remaining members, Mr. and Mrs. Montgomery. Eliza's parents refused to give up hope. As it turned out, they were right to believe that their daughter was alive and well and would be home soon. Fourteen days and several hours after first going missing, Eliza walked up to the front door of her family's home. She was disoriented, exhausted, and covered in dirt, but physically she was unscathed. Unfortunately, the same cannot be said of her parents.

That morning, before Eliza returned home, Mrs. Montgomery's sister stopped by with a casserole for later that night. She says she knew that the last two weeks had been hard for her sister and brother-in-law and that they had been skipping meals to search for their daughter. No one answered when she knocked on the door so she took the casserole inside and then crossed the yard. As she approached the trees, she thought she heard a child laughing. She ran toward the sound, but instead of finding her niece, she found Ben and Jennifer Montgomery, dead. The county coroner ruled their deaths an accident. They appeared to have been victims of an animal attack.

As for Eliza Montgomery, she has not spoken since her return but she is safe and unharmed. Eliza was placed in the custody of her aunt.

A memorial service for Ben and Jennifer is scheduled for Saturday at 10:30 AM.

13

In the week after their last trip to Madame Ethelinda's shop, Mason and Amber barely spoke. When they did, the conversation primarily consisted of Amber asking Mason how he could have kept the presence of two more ghosts from her and Mason responding that he didn't want to worry her or that he thought he was going crazy and that they were not real. They each took a turn yelling and then they returned to not speaking to each other.

Their most recent shouting match happened just before Amber left for work. The picture frames on the wall in the living room rattled as she slammed the door on her way out.

"Tough break," Ruby said. She almost sounded sincere but the upturned corners of her mouth gave her away.

"Why won't you just tell me what you want?" Mason said.

"I don't want anything, love."

"Bullshit. That old gypsy said you all needed something from me because you're disturbed. Just tell me what it is so I can get rid of you."

"You saw how I died, yeah? 'Course I'm disturbed. But I don't need anything from you."

"Timmy?"

"N-nothing for m-m-me, thanks."

"I hate you both. Okay, what about her?" Mason waved a hand toward Eliza, who was standing in the doorway between the dining room and the kitchen, bouncing her ball. "Any thoughts?"

Thanks to Ruby and Madame Ethelinda, he knew the girl's name. And that—*somehow*—he used to be her. But that was it. Eliza still had not said a single word. She just stared and played with that damn ball.

"W-well," Timmy said, "she's a little kid. H-have you tried playing with her?"

"Brilliant," Ruby said. "That's exactly what I told him, innit?"

"Y-yes b-but d-did he ever t-try it?" Timmy's stutter always seemed more pronounced when he talked to Ruby. Being stuck with her for all those years must have taken its toll. Mason had to do whatever it took to get rid of them. God forbid he end up like Timmy—a ghost with a stutter who needed an inhaler to function despite no longer actually needing to breathe.

Eliza began to bounce the ball harder as Mason approached her. Her eyes narrowed. Mason reached out and grabbed the ball. She lunged at him, grabbing onto his wrist with both of her hands. Her fingernails dug into his skin, the touch of her hands like dry ice. He took the ball with his other hand and threw it down the hall, hoping that she would chase after it and let go of his arm.

As Eliza sped down the hallway after her ball, Mason thought of Jacoby. How many times had he done the exact same thing to get Jacoby to leave him alone? Mason's eyes filled with tears. He blinked them back and looked down at his arm. He could almost hear the skin blistering where she had touched him. There were ten small slivers of blood where her nails had pierced his skin and maroon bruises wrapped around his wrist.

Eliza caught up to the ball and held it with both hands. She hunkered down, protecting the ball, and rolled it inside her cupped hands. Eliza stayed at the far end of the hallway and hissed at Mason.

"Looks like she doesn't wanna play," Ruby said.

"Help me out here," Mason said. "I just want to get my life back."

"Some life," Timmy said out of the corner of his mouth.

"What was that?" Mason snapped at him.

"If sh-she doesn't w-w-want to play, m-maybe th-there's a c-c-clue in the w-way she died."

"Now there's an idea," Ruby said. Timmy flinched as she patted him on the back. Ruby smiled at that. "How did she die?"

"No clue," Mason said.

"What about the dream?"

Mason shrugged.

"You *did* have a dream about her, didn't you?"

"Sure. But it wasn't like the ones I had of you guys. I didn't... I mean, *she* didn't die in it."

"Wh-what was it about then?"

"Her ball. Kind of..."

"Go on," Ruby said. For the first time, she seemed truly interested in something other than pestering Mason or Timmy.

"She... *I* was chasing the ball through a bunch of trees. And then a car was coming and I thought I was going to get hit, so I closed my eyes. Then there was this laugh. And a drill. And then I woke up."

"That's got to be it then!" Ruby jumped—or rather floated off the ground—as she spoke. "She doesn't know how she died. I love a good mystery. Don't you?"

"Not this one," Mason said.

He grabbed his cell phone to call Amber. It rang four times. He was about to hang up—he assumed that she was screening his call—when she answered.

"What?" Amber said.

"I think we figured it out."

"We? What did we figure out?"

"Eliza. She doesn't know how she died." Mason felt relieved and hopeful for the first time in months.

"Oh? So by *we,* you mean you and your secret ghost pals?"

"Well... yes. But we know how to get rid of her now." He had not expected that he would have to convince Amber that this was good news. "We know what she needs."

"Okay," Amber said. "And how exactly do you and your friends plan on figuring out how this little girl died when you don't even know when she lived?"

"I don't know," Mason said. His hope began to fade.

"That's what I thought," said Amber. She hung up the phone.

Mason's mouth hung open. He slid down the side of the couch until he was sitting on the floor with his legs stretched out in front of him. He held his phone in his lap and let his head roll forward on his neck until his chin was touching his chest. Ruby and Timmy did not say a word. Eliza crept back toward the living room and when she saw Mason sitting on the floor, she began to laugh.

...

That evening, Amber came in and tossed her purse onto the couch. She did not even look at Mason. Instead, she went straight to the closet in their bedroom. When Mason caught up to her, there were shoes strewn about the bedroom floor. She had tossed them out of her way. Amber had a storage bin buried at the bottom of the closet. The lid was off and she was digging through old photos and report cards.

"Are we going to talk about earlier?" Mason asked from the doorway. He stopped before entering the bedroom. He didn't want to get too close until he knew what her reaction might be.

Amber ignored him. She kept digging through the box of childhood memories. After a couple of minutes she stood up, holding something, and walked right past Mason. Still, she had not said a word.

Mason followed her to the living room. Amber sat on the couch and placed an old yearbook on the coffee table in front of her. She flipped through several pages of signatures and notes from her childhood friends. Then she took her phone and dialed a number. She held the phone up to her ear and walked into the kitchen. Mason looked at the open yearbook. One signature stood out. It was in the center of the page and had a big circle around it.

Keep in touch—Bill.

There was a phone number below his name. It was that number Amber dialed. He could not hear much of her conversation, but it was brief. She came out of the kitchen holding a notepad and dialed another number. Mason was able to hear that conversation.

"Hi, Bill. I don't know if you remember me but we went to high school together... Yeah, Amber... Good, good. I got your number from your parents... Yeah. You wrote it in my yearbook... I was hoping we could get together... Lunch tomorrow sounds great. See you then."

***

Bill Hamilton had been a bit of a laughing stock when they were growing up. He weighed a hundred and five pounds all through high school, always had a neatly trimmed bowl cut that his mom gave him, and his glasses did not stay up. He walked with his shoulders slumped and he kept his books in a wheeled suitcase—a backpack was too heavy to carry.

For a while, Bill and Amber were close friends. They bonded over their love of all things paranormal. Every time a group project was assigned, they paired up and found a way to turn it into a report on aliens or ghosts or latent psychic abilities. But as they grew older,

Amber's hobbies diversified—she became interested in volleyball and cheerleading and gossiping with the other girls—and they grew apart.

The summer after they graduated high school, Bill began producing his own public-access television show. He called it *Urban Phenomena with Bill Hamilton*. It started off in the *five a.m.* time slot, but it moved to a new time when the host of another show went off to college and then his show really took off—by public-access standards at least. After the station shut down, he turned the show into a podcast and renamed it *What in the World?*

Within eight months, his show peaked as the fourth most popular podcast in the country and it had not been out of the top twenty since.

Amber filled Mason in on Bill's show on their way to meet him for lunch—Amber never missed an episode, even though they had not spoken since high school. She was upset with Mason for keeping Ruby and Timmy a secret, but she was glad that they came up with this idea. If nothing else, it would be nice to reconnect with Bill after so many years.

Overall, lunch with Bill was uneventful. Amber gushed about what a big fan she was and how she could not believe how long it had been since they had seen each other. Bill went on and on about how much better his life had been since high school.

Mason sat back in the booth and rolled his eyes. A waitress brought the check to the table. Amber and Bill both reached for it and did the usual who-is-going-to-pay dance.

"I called you. The least I can do is pay for lunch."

"All right. Fine," Bill conceded. "But only if you tell me the real reason you called. It's been great catching up but nobody decides to look someone up after eight years unless they want something."

"You're right. We need your help," Amber said.

Mason filled Bill in on the story so far, beginning with Jacoby freaking out at the asylum and finishing with the revelation from Madame Ethelinda about Mason's past lives.

"From what we know of the other two, we think the girl died violently but she doesn't talk like they do. And she doesn't look fully human. That's why Amber thought you might be able to help. All we know is her name. Eliza Montgomery."

"You left out the part where that creepy little bitch killed my dog," Amber said.

Bill made a note of her name in his phone as Mason told him about what happened at the campground.

"That wasn't her," Bill said.

"Of course it was," Amber said. "Who else could it have been?"

"I don't know. But it couldn't have been her. If your gypsy friend is right, and I trust that you believe she is, then this girl is the ghost of one of Mason's past lives. What I like to call a spirit remnant.

"I don't have much experience with them, but what I have found in my research is that spirit remnants latch onto the current incarnation of their soul for a reason—anything from needing help finding closure to wanting to hang onto the real world instead of moving on—but they absolutely cannot manipulate solid objects.

"Sure, they might send a gust of wind your way or make a few lights flicker but that's about it. There is no way she could have run a spear through your dog."

With that, Bill Hamilton pushed his glasses up the bridge of his nose and stood up from the table.

"Thanks for lunch," he said. "Amber, it was good to see you again. Mason..." he tapped the side of his phone against the table. "I'll look into this for you. See what I can do to help."

A bell rang as he opened the diner's door and again as it swung closed behind him.

"What do we do now?" Mason asked Amber.

"We wait."

14

Waiting was not an easy thing to do. Mason spent the next week obsessively checking his phone, hearing chimes and feeling buzzing in his pocket that was not there. Whenever he saw Amber, he asked if Bill had called. Her answer was always the same. *Not yet.*

Ruby and Timmy had taken to playing cribbage, though where they found cards and a cribbage board with that same sort of glow as them—blue instead of pink or brown—was anybody's guess. They still bickered like siblings, but they had mostly left Mason alone. Eliza just stayed in the shadows bouncing her ball. It didn't matter that Mason knew she couldn't hurt him, the sound of that ball and her wide-eyed glare made his back sweat. He tried not to think about what would happen if he couldn't help her. He might not have gone insane yet but if she stayed with him for the rest of his life, it would only be a matter of time.

Amber walked into the living room where Mason was sitting on the couch. He immediately asked her if she had heard anything, expecting to get the same response as usual.

"Yes," Amber said. "Let's go."

She tossed Mason his jacket and went out to the car to wait for him.

"Bill found an old newspaper article about Eliza Montgomery and her parents. She went to live with her aunt after her parents died. After a little more digging he found out that she was sent to the Farm by her aunt." Amber said once they were in the car.

"That's great. Explains why she found me when we were there."

"Exactly."

"And we are going to talk to the aunt?" Mason asked.

"No. She died fifteen years ago."

"So where are we going?"

"The library. One of the old nurses works there now. Everyone else who worked at the asylum is either dead or left town after it shut down. "

Mason leaned his head against the window and closed his eyes as Amber backed the car out of the driveway.

***

He was chasing the ball through the trees again. Every turn brought his hand closer to grabbing it. He came out of the trees and stretched out his arm. The tips of his fingers could feel the red fuzz.

Almost got it. Then the lights came. A truck. He closed his eyes. The tires squealed and the smell of hot rubber drifted into his nostrils.

Everything went quiet. Everything stayed dark.

The burning rubber smell was replaced with lemon-scented bleach.

Mason opened his eyes. Everything around him was white. The walls, the floors, the bed in the corner. All of it.

The room he was standing in was almost empty. There was just a small cot in the corner with white sheets, a thin white blanket, and a single pillow in a white pillowcase.

He made his way over to the small window opposite the door. It looked out on a large lawn with a sidewalk winding through it. There were rows of corn and wheat and apple trees. Several people were outside—some in hospital gowns, some in shorts and tee-shirts—dressed all in white. There was a graveyard with grieving family members visiting lost loved ones.

The door opened behind him. Mason turned. A large man wearing a tight white tee-shirt and white shorts (with a white belt, white socks, and white shoes) pushed a wheelchair into the room.

"Okay, Eliza. It's time for your treatment," the large man said.

The man called him Eliza. Mason knew that was wrong. But it didn't *feel* wrong. He had a nagging suspicion that he should be asking the man something. Something important. Something just out of reach. He searched the corners of his mind for what it could be but it stayed just out of reach. Like the ball.

Where's my ball? That's what he wanted to ask the big man. He thought the words, but his mouth did not move.

"Come on sweetie. Sit down. The doctor is waiting." The big man's voice was deep and smooth and Mason trusted it. He sat down in the wheelchair.

"That's my girl," the big man said. He smiled at Mason. Mason wanted to smile back, but again his face did not move. The big man leaned down so that Mason could feel the warm air blowing from his nostrils. He lowered his voice and reached into the back pocket of his shorts.

"Don't tell anyone, but I brought you a surprise. I know you must be nervous for today. I thought this might help." He handed a red tennis ball to Mason.

Mason cupped the ball in his left hand and stroked it with his right. He smiled. And this time his mouth did what his brain told it to do. He twisted his head up to look at the big man.

"There's that beautiful smile." The big man backed out of the room with the wheelchair and they started down the hallway. "You really should try to smile more." His voice was hypnotic. Mason thought the big man was right. He should smile more. He kept petting his ball in his lap and grinned all the way down the hallway.

The big man pushed him past all of the rooms in the east wing. A few of the doors were closed. Those were the rooms of the patients who were not allowed to go outside on their own. They waited inside for someone to come get them. Most of the doors were open. It was almost lunchtime. That meant that everyone who was not scheduled for treatment was out doing their chores—all of the chores had to be finished before anyone was allowed to eat.

Mason's stomach growled at the thought of lunch. The big man laughed.

"Don't worry. I'll make sure you get all you can eat after your treatment. Okay?"

He nodded.

"But right now the doctor is waiting for us. I'd lose my job if I didn't take you straight to him. And I can't afford to lose this job."

Mason nodded again, but the smile began to fade from his face. He looked down at the ball in his lap so the big man wouldn't see. They turned at the end of the hall and passed the reception desk. As they continued out the front door, the sunlight made Mason's head hurt. He closed his eyes.

The air smelled familiar—like horses and hay and corn and wheat—like home. The big man pushed Mason up a ramp into another building. The comforting smell of summer air was replaced with the sting of ammonia. Mason opened his eyes. They were in a building he had never been in before. The doctor stood in the middle of the room with two nurses next to him. There was another big man standing behind a chair with straps on its arms and legs.

Mason tucked the ball into the waistband of his own white shorts and placed his hands over the bulge. He hoped that he hid it before anyone saw. He was not allowed to have the ball here, it was too angry of a color. At least that was what the mean lady at the front desk had said when she took it away from him. The next day she brought a foam baseball to Mason's room and gave it to him with a smile like that would make everything better. But it wasn't *his* ball.

The new big man stepped around the strappy chair and grabbed Mason's wrist. When Mason refused to get to his feet, the big man pulled Mason up by his arm. He lifted Mason until his feet were at least a foot off of the ground.

Mason kicked his feet violently and thrashed his body around. The ball fell from his waistband and bounced across the room. Mason's big man grabbed him by the ankles and together, the two men set him down in the strappy chair.

Mason stopped kicking and let his big man secure his ankles, after which he raised up so that he was face-to-face with Mason. He pulled his lips to the side in an *I'm sorry* sort of way and then pushed Mason's head back against the chair and strapped that down too.

The ball came to a stop against the doctor's foot. He rolled it under his shoe a couple of times before kicking it to the corner of the room.

"Tsk, tsk, tsk," said the doctor. He turned toward Mason and squatted onto a stool. He wheeled himself over to the strappy chair and smiled as he waited for a nurse to bring him a silver tray. Mason was flanked by a big man on either side. The nurse with the tray sat next to the doctor. The other nurse came over and stood right behind him.

The doctor picked a drill up off the tray and smiled at Mason.

"This is for your own good," he said. "It is going to bring you back to us."

The doctor kept talking but Mason could only make out bits and pieces of what he said over the sound of the drill.

"...aunt wants... home... don't you..."

The doctor pushed the tip of the drill into the side of Mason's forehead. Mason screamed. The sound of the drill began bouncing around inside his head. Shards of bone shot out behind the drill.

The doctor pulled the drill out and the nurse behind him quickly pressed something white against the hole in Mason's head. He said something that Mason couldn't hear over the echo of the drill still inside his skull. Both of the nurses laughed. Then the doctor wiped off the drill and did the same thing to the other side of Mason's head.

Mason tried to focus on his ball sitting in the corner of the room but it became a red blur in a sea of white. The doctor put the drill back on the tray and picked up something else. Mason could not see what it was. But he could feel it.

The doctor put it into one of the holes in his head and rotated it inside his brain. The pressure was unbearable. It felt as though Mason's head was about to split in two. Something inside his brain popped and then everything went black.

***

Amber drove over a pothole.

(something inside his brain popped)

Mason woke up.

"Sorry," she said. "It looked like you needed the sleep."

"I did. And I think I know how Eliza died."

"That's great. You can run your theory by her nurse. We're here." Amber opened her door and stepped out of the car.

Mason flipped down the visor above his seat and looked in the mirror. His eyes were bloodshot with dark purple rings around them. His bangs were soaked and looked like they had been super-glued to his forehead.

"I'll catch up to you," he said.

The top of Ruby's face appeared in the mirror next to his. She was sitting in the driver's seat and leaned over to get a better look at Mason in the mirror.

"Good call. You look like total rubbish."

A hearty laugh came from the back seat followed immediately by a fit of coughing and wheezing. Timmy scrambled for the inhaler in his pocket and took a puff.

Mason turned his head in the mirror. He rubbed his fingers over his temples. When he was convinced that he did not have holes drilled in his brain, he took a handful of tissues and tried to scrub the sweat out of his hair.

"What do you want now?" Mason asked his ghosts.

"Didn't you miss us?" Ruby said.

"Y - y - yeah. Wh-what makes you th-think we want s-something?" Timmy added.

"Sure," Mason said, rolling his eyes. He turned back to the mirror and ran the comb through his hair.

"So, how have you been?" Ruby asked.

"Fantastic," Mason said flatly. "Can't you tell?"

“Th-that’s great,” Timmy said.

“No, it’s not great you moron. ‘Course he isn’t fantastic. Just lookit him.”

Mason laughed. He couldn’t help himself.

“What gave me away? That I haven’t had a decent night’s sleep in months? Or that I just got to experience first-hand what it’s like to have my brain split in half by a doctor who was telling jokes while he did it? Or maybe that I’m about to go meet someone who was there when it happened? Or, I know. Could it be that I’m talking to two ghosts about all of this who—by the way—just happen to both be me and were also both murdered?”

“L-l-lobotomy huh? Th-that’s no f-fun. Doctors offered me one s-since they th-thought my a-asthma was all in m-my h-head. No w-way was I going to try it.”

“If there’s nothing else you want to add, I’m going to go with my girlfriend to interview one of the people who killed Eliza.”

“Sounds like a fun date,” Ruby said.

Mason caught up to Amber on the other side of the parking lot. Bill was standing next to her.

“Took you long enough,” he said to Mason.

Mason grunted and nodded in his direction. The three of them headed up the walkway to the library. Bill took the lead. Amber rubbed Mason’s shoulder and ran her hand down his arm. She took his hand in hers and they followed Bill in silence.

The library was nothing like Mason remembered. The reading tables that had taken up the majority of the building were now covered with monitors and keyboards. Instead of reading, kids sat at the tables to play video games. Instead of a rack filled with recent issues of newspapers and magazines, there was a pair of computers with web browsers open to online subscriptions of *The New York Times, National Geographic,* and *Time.*

There were a half dozen people in the library and not one had a book open—or even within ten feet of them.

The librarian's desk was on the back wall of the library. As they walked between the stacks, the library began to feel more familiar. The air still smelled like old paper and stale leather. And it was still quiet. That hadn't changed.

A woman sat at the librarian's desk. Her gray hair was pulled back but enough strands hadn't made it into her bun that the top of her head looked like an old, frayed rope. Her cheeks looked like they were barely holding on to her cheekbones. She looked up at them over her half-moon reading glasses. Her eyes lit up when she smiled at them.

"How can I help you folks?"

"Well..." Bill leaned down and pushed his glasses up the bridge of his nose as he squinted at the name tag pinned to the librarian's blue knit sweater. "Dorothy. You are actually just the gal we were hoping to talk to. You see..." He adjusted his glasses again. "We have been trying to do some research on the Farm, but other than the rumors and ghost stories all the kids tell each other we haven't had much luck. We heard you used to work there."

"Yes I did. The Farm. Wow, I haven't thought of that place in years." She shook her head slightly to keep from drifting off with the memory. The corners of her mouth were turned up—remembering her old job fondly—but Mason thought there was something else behind that smile. It looked uneasy.

"So what do you say?" asked Amber. "Would you mind if we ask you a few questions?"

Dorothy looked around the library. There were two young boys—maybe twelve years old—playing a game on one of the computers. A teenage girl was taking a sip from the drinking fountain near the restrooms. A couple of high school sweethearts held hands as they walked out into the parking lot.

"Not here," the librarian said. She placed a laminated picture of a clock on her desk and moved the hands to *four thirty-five*.

Dorothy stood up and led them through a door marked *Employees Only*. The room was filled with carts, most of them empty. The few that weren't had piles of books on them waiting to be reshelved. So, at least some people still used the library for reading.

"What would you like to know?" Dorothy said. "I can't promise that I can answer all of your questions. It was so long ago and I don't think of that place often. But I will tell you whatever I am able."

Dorothy-the-librarian used to be Dorothy-the-nurse. She had been the youngest employee at the Farm. She worked there for three and a half years before the asylum was forced to shut down.

"Why were you shut down?" Amber asked.

"We believed we were helping people. Yes, sometimes they didn't survive the treatments—I'm sure you've heard about our on-site graveyard—but those people needed help and we gave it to them as best we could.

"Fifty-seven or fifty-eight years ago, some people got it in their heads that we were doing terrible things to our patients. They said our treatments were essentially torture and that we would lock people up for conditions that did not exist as long as someone was willing to pay their bill."

"Was that true?" Bill asked. "Were you torturing people?"

"Of course not. Some of the treatments may have been controversial, but they weren't torture. The doctors were trying to heal minds. It was an admirable goal. The rest of us were there because we believed in that mission. We were trying to make the world a better place."

"Then why did you need a cemetery?" Amber asked.

"Like I said, some of the treatments were controversial. They involved more risk, but gave a chance to the patients that did not respond to anything else. And we only tried them with the blessing of the patient's family. For some, it was worth the risk."

"Worth the risk? You killed Eliza. But it's okay because it was worth the risk?" Mason blurted out.

"I've never killed anyone," Dorothy snapped. "And I think you need to leave now."

"No. Wait," Bill said. "Mason hasn't been sleeping well. What he meant to say was that we were hoping you remembered a young girl. Eliza Montgomery. She would have been a patient there about sixty years ago. She went missing and her parents died before they found her."

"She always carried a red ball with her," Amber added.

"The girl with the ball, that's right. I remember her. She was one of the first patients admitted after I started working there. One of the orderlies almost lost an eye when he had to take that ball from her. We did not allow personal effects in the hospital."

"Is there anything else you remember about her?" Bill asked.

"She did not say a single word while she was with us. That's why her aunt brought her to the Farm. She had become completely nonverbal. We tried everything to get her to talk—about what happened to her, her parents, anything—but nothing worked. She always worked hard, on her treatments and her chores, but she just never seemed to be all the way there. It was like she was somewhere else. After a few months, Dr. Jefferson suggested we try a lobotomy."

Mason was getting tired of hearing about how great that place was when he had seen what happened there. He rubbed the inside corners of his eyes with his thumb and forefinger and shook his head.

"She wouldn't talk? That's it? That's why you drilled into her head and killed her?" Mason snapped.

"I told you, I've never killed anyone. Yes. She was lobotomized. And yes. She died. But not until a year later. The lobotomy helped. She was still nonverbal but her demeanor improved. She smiled more and was clearly less worried about whatever it was that had caused her condition. And now you need to leave. I won't stand here being called a murderer by people who are wanting my help."

"But—" Bill started.

"Go." Dorothy pointed an arthritic finger at the door. Mason's eyes narrowed. He tried to stand his ground, but Amber grabbed his elbow and pulled him out of the room.

"Sorry. Thank you for your time," she said as the three of them left the room. Mason was still watching the old woman as the door swung shut. Dorothy buried her face in her hands.

Ruby and Timmy were playing cribbage in the backseat when Amber and Mason got back to the car.

"What was that?" Amber said as the car door shut behind them.

Ruby quit pegging mid-move and poked her head between the two front seats. She looked over at Mason with a smirk.

"That bad was it?" she said.

"I don't care what she says. That old lady killed me."

"You aren't dead. Do you mean Eliza? How could you possibly know that?"

"She told me." Amber raised an eyebrow. "Or showed me. Whatever. I lived it. I was her. That nurse held the gauze to my head while some doctor popped my brain in half."

"That's what was supposed to happen. It was a lobotomy." Amber was still waiting for a good excuse.

"That's how this works. I have a dream where I relive their deaths," Mason said.

"N-not exactly," Timmy said from the back seat. Mason snapped his head around the seat.

"What do you mean *not exactly*? You suffocated watching a store get robbed. I'm pretty sure she got carved up by Jack the Ripper. And Eliza had her brain drilled."

Yes, yes, and y-yes. But that doesn't m-m-mean that is what killed her."

"That's right," Ruby said. "We can show you anything we please. Just is easiest to replay the last thing we remember, is all. That's why you got to see our deaths. Doesn't mean you saw hers."

"I hate when you do that," Amber said. "What are they saying?"

"She showed me a memory, but it wasn't how she died," Mason said.

"You think? That's what Dorothy was trying to tell us before you accused her of murder." Amber's phone beeped. "Bill wants to meet up at the diner again. He has an idea."

***

A waitress carried a tray with a shot of whiskey, a beer, and two milkshakes to their table. She set the strawberry one down in front of Amber. Bill got vanilla. Mason took the shot and placed the empty glass back on her tray as she set his beer on a coaster.

"It's really not that crazy of an idea," Amber said, swirling her straw in the cold pink drink after the waitress went back to the kitchen.

Mason responded by drinking half of his pint in one gulp.

"Think about it. That librarian could have finished telling us what happened to Eliza, but I don't think it matters if she died a year after the lobotomy. Maybe her death isn't what she needs your help with," Bill said. Mason finished the rest of his beer and belched.

“So what then? How am I supposed to get rid of her if she doesn’t want to know how she died?”

“Figure out what no one could while she was alive.” Bill slid his phone across the table to Mason. On it was an old newspaper article. “She went missing for two weeks. Nobody knows what happened during that time and after she came back, she did not say another word for the rest of her life. I think that’s the key. She either needs your help to remember what happened, or she wants you to know so that you can tell her story in a way that she was never able to.”

Amber took the phone from Mason and quickly skimmed the article.

“It says here she went missing in the forest by her house, but it doesn’t give an address,” Amber said.

“Leave that to me,” Bill said. “I know a guy.”

The waitress returned to their table and the three of them ordered dinner. Throughout the meal Bill and Amber reminisced about high school and the paranormal research club that they had attempted to start—it never took off because no one else joined. Mason focused on his burger and on trying to tune out Timmy and Ruby. They were discussing which foods they missed the most and arguing over whether Mason’s burger came with fries or chips.

By the time the waitress brought the check to the table, Bill had received an email with the address of Eliza’s house.

15

Amber was not able to get much sleep that night. Mason spent the night tossing and turning and letting out random bursts of laughter and screams. She lay awake until Bill pulled into the driveway the next morning and honked twice.

"Let's go," she said, shaking Mason awake. She threw a zip-up hoodie and a pair of jeans at Mason before he had even opened his eyes. He groaned and nodded, waving a hand for her to go.

He pulled on the pants and sweatshirt and went out to Bill's car, carrying his shoes. He sat down behind the driver's seat in the middle row of Bill's black, late-model Escalade. Before he could bend down to put on his shoes, he heard Ruby clearing her throat. Timmy was already sitting behind Amber, she was standing outside Mason's door.

Mason slid over. Bill handed a cup of coffee to Mason and backed out of the driveway.

"Thanks," Mason said.

"It's early. I figured we could all use some caffeine."

The house that Eliza had lived in was just over an hour out of town. It was a decent sized rancher that had probably been very nice when she had lived there. Whoever lived there now had not done much to keep it up and the age of the home showed.

"This place looks like a dump," Mason said after swallowing the last gulp of his lukewarm coffee.

"Maybe. But we aren't here to see the house," Bill said. "We want to check out the forest on the back of the property."

The house sat in the middle of a seven-acre lot, most of which was flat and covered in grass. The property line behind the house, however, extended into the edge of a forest. Highway 63 ran through the trees at the property line and the forest continued on the other side of the road.

"That's where she went missing?" Amber asked.

"Maybe. At the very least we know it was the last place anyone saw her," Bill said. He looked at Mason in the rearview mirror. "Is she with us?" He whispered as if the sound of his voice might frighten away her ghost.

Mason looked into the back seat. Eliza was sitting with her feet pulled in and her knees tucked up to her chest. Her hands were clasped around the ball in front of her legs, her sharp teeth chewed on her lips.

"Yes," Mason said.

Bill slowed the car as they approached the house.

"I think your friend might be onto something here," Ruby said. She tilted her head back toward Eliza. She had dropped her ball and wrapped her hands around her shins.

Bill and Amber got out of the car. Mason, Ruby, and Timmy followed them to the porch. Eliza stayed in her seat.

"S-something is n-not right w-with this place," Timmy said.

"You said it. Poor girl sounds like a kettle," Ruby said. Eliza had started making a hissing sound—not the aggressive, territorial hiss that she used when someone tried to take her ball. It was more like when someone pinches the neck of a balloon and lets the air out.

The house was silent when they reached the front door. Amber knocked. More silence. She waited thirty seconds and knocked again. Still nothing. She tried the doorbell. They heard the chime echo through the empty house.

"I don't think anyone is home," Mason said.

"I didn't expect them to be. It's better that no one knows we are here."

"You want us to sneak onto their property?" Amber said.

"He's right," Mason said. "What would we say if somebody wanted to know why we were here? We couldn't tell them that I'm being haunted by the girl who used to live in their house. They would slam the door in our faces."

"At least," Bill said. "Or call the cops. Either way, our investigation would be over." Bill and Mason backed down the steps and made their way across the yard toward the trees.

"I still don't like it. It doesn't seem right," Amber said but she followed them anyway.

In the summer, the yard was probably a luscious green, now it was yellow-brown and frozen to the dirt below it.

As they got closer to the trees, Mason saw four rocks lined up, all about five feet apart. No grass grew in front of the rocks. A mound of mulch around the base of a barron rosebush sat to the left of each stone.

"Graves?" Bill asked as they got closer. Each rock had a name carved into it. *Spot, Max, Dino, Rover.*

"Dogs," Mason said.

Amber shivered—not from the wind. Ruby and Timmy each had an arm around Eliza. They dragged her across the lawn. When they caught up to Mason standing next to the homemade headstones, Eliza twisted out of their grasp and took off into the trees.

"W-we'll get h-her," Timmy told Mason.

"So what are we looking for?" Mason asked Bill.

"I think we will know when we find it."

"How? Do you have some special equipment or something?" Amber asked.

"I don't. Mason does."

"I didn't bring anything."

"You brought Eliza," Bill said. "If we find what we need, she will let us know."

With that, the three of them entered the forest. Up ahead, Timmy and Ruby were with Eliza. She had calmed enough that they did not need to hold her anymore.

They walked farther into the woods, following a narrow trail that had been worn over time. Mason recognized the path. He had followed it in his dreams.

Mason took the lead. He wound them along the trail, deeper into the forest. The sun was high, the sky clear, but the light around them was disappearing. The path narrowed. The trees grew thicker.

And then the light was back. They were standing on the side of the highway. Mason stopped. This was where the dreams became nightmares. It was as far as he could lead them. He looked at Eliza.

Her eyes were wide. She started rocking, her hands still wringing themselves into her ball. She shook her head back and forth. Eliza's eyes darted briefly across the road.

Mason led them up the bank on the other side of the highway and looked back over his shoulder at Eliza. Once again her eyes darted to the side.

"This way," Mason said.

"Lookit him," Ruby said to Timmy, "trying to take credit for something a little girl is doing."

Mason ignored her and kept going. After a few more steps, Mason froze. Somewhere in the distance he could hear a child laughing. A gust of wind swirled the sound around his head. He knew that laugh.

"What was that?" Amber said.

"There shouldn't be anyone out here except us," said Bill. "That house is the only thing bordering this forest. It's too cold for campers and hunting season ended last week."

"You heard that? That's the same laugh as in my dream."

"I'll go check it out. You two keep going."

"Now what?" Amber asked Mason after Bill was gone.

He looked at Eliza. She had curled up on the ground.

"I don't know," Mason said. He started walking, watching Eliza with each step he took for some kind of reaction. *Nothing*.

They turned behind a tree and kept walking. Mason continued looking back even though Eliza, Ruby, and Timmy were no longer in sight. Amber stopped.

"I want to talk to you about something." Amber looked around. "Are we alone?"

Mason looked back the way they had come. The ghosts were out of sight but he could still hear them arguing.

"How w-would I know what's wrong with h-her?"

"You're the one who had all the medical issues. Can't you fix her with your inhaler?"

"I have asthma. N-not wh-whatever this is."

Mason forced a smile at Amber. "Alone enough," he said.

"Okay... well... I've been thinking a lot about what Dr. Phillips said. Once we get this whole past-life thing behind us, I think it might be for the best if we took some time apart to—"

"You want to break up?" Mason interrupted.

"No. No, of course not. I just want us to both take some time to think about what we want our future to look like so we can get on the same page. And I think the only way to do that would be to take a step back so that we can think clearly. I can stay with my mom for a few days."

"You don't have to do that," Mason said.

"Yes I do. You need to be able to decide what it is that you want and where you think we are headed. And I can't be there while you are doing that."

Mason started to respond but he was cut off by another laugh. It was right above them. Then it sounded miles away. The sound came at them from everywhere and nowhere. Mason and Amber spun around, looking through the trees to find its source. A branch moved on the tree up ahead of them, but the laugh was far off in the distance behind them.

"Did you see that?" Amber said.

"Must be a squirrel or something. Whatever is making that noise sounds like it is long gone," Mason said.

"H-h-help! H-help!" Timmy swung around a tree and doubled over. He patted himself frantically, looking for his inhaler.

"What's wrong?" Mason asked him. Amber raised an eyebrow at Mason. "I'll be right back," he told her. Mason jogged back to the tree that Timmy was hanging onto.

"S-something wrong... E-Eliza." Timmy stammered and raised the inhaler to his lips.

"You know you don't actually need that, right?" Mason said as he ran past Timmy. Timmy scowled and waved his hand as he squeezed the inhaler and sucked the powder into his lungs.

Ruby was down on one knee patting Eliza on the back, but keeping her body as far away from the girl as possible. She stood up as Mason approached and stepped back.

"Your turn, love."

"What's happening?" Mason asked.

"Haven't the slightest. Ever since that laughing started up, she's gone all to pot."

Looking down at Eliza, Mason thought of the old TV he had bought at a garage sale when he was seven. It had rabbit ears and if they weren't positioned just right, the screen filled with colored bars and static. The picture would stay frozen behind the bars and snow until there was a strong enough signal for the image to change. Then it would jump to a new image and freeze again. That is what Eliza seemed to be doing on the forest floor.

She was alternating between the ghost that Mason knew—gray skin, sharp teeth, greasy hair—and a tomboyish little girl with her red hair pulled back in a ponytail underneath a backward baseball cap, green eyes and freckles, overalls, and a pinstripe Yankees jacket.

"How do we stop it?" Mason asked although he knew there would be no answer. If Ruby had any idea about what was happening to Eliza, she would not have needed him. The two of them stood over Eliza, watching as the girl she used to be turned into the monster that they were used to and back again.

"It means we're onto something being out here, right?" Mason looked at Ruby. She shrugged. "I mean, it has to. But what do we do now?"

Another laugh echoed through the trees. This time it sounded even farther away. Eliza stopped changing. She was back to her usual appearance—the one Mason was more familiar with. That was good. It might be worse being haunted by a normal six-year-old.

The laugh faded and was immediately replaced by a piercing scream from just around the bend in the trail—from where Mason had left Amber.

He forgot all about Eliza. About Ruby. About why he was out in this forest and whether or not Bill was going to find anything. He left Amber alone and something happened. Nothing else mattered.

He ran straight past Timmy, who had just gotten back to them. He jumped over a rock on the trail and swung around the tree that Timmy had used for support. Amber wasn't there. This was where he had left her, but she was gone.

Mason called out for Amber. Her name bounced around the trees and echoed throughout the forest. The only sound that returned was the rustling of branches in the wind.

"Amber? Amber!" *Nothing.*

Something crunched under his foot. Her phone. The screen cracked when he stepped on it, but he could see that the dialer was pulled up. Whatever happened to her, happened fast. She had not even had time to press the first number.

Mason fell to his knees and wrapped his arms around his head.

"Amber? Mason? What's going on?" Bill ran up the trail. He was dripping sweat and out of breath—not quite as bad as Timmy had looked when he had come to get Mason, but close.

"I heard a scream. Where's Amber?" They had all turned on the location sharing on their phones before they left Bill's car and he had come running when he heard the scream.

"She's gone," Mason said.

***

"We looked out there for hours," Mason said. "There was no sign of her anywhere. How are old newspapers going to help us find her?"

"We were close to figuring out what happened to Eliza. You said as much yourself. I think the same thing just happened to Amber."

"I don't care what you think. We have to go to the police."

"We can't. They won't be able to help us. But we don't have to. I found something."

Bill turned his computer monitor so Mason could see it. He had found several articles about that property—missing kids, accidental deaths—and they all had one thing in common. Someone always reported hearing laughter in the distance.

"How does that help us?"

"All of those disappearances were just like at Amber's. My guess is that they're the same as Eliza's, too," Bill said. "No bodies were ever found after someone went missing."

"And?"

"And Eliza came back. That means whatever happened to those missing kids, they were probably kept alive. Like Eliza. That means Amber would be too. We can still find her."

Mason wanted to believe Bill. He had to believe Bill. It was the only chance he had to find Amber. But—

"How could all these stories be related? There are some here that are almost a hundred years old?"

"What's your point?" Bill said.

"There's no way that it could be the same person every time."

"I don't think we are dealing with a person, Mason. Do you? After everything you've seen, do you really still think a person is responsible for all of this? You're being haunted by three different ghosts that are all past versions of yourself. Why can't you accept that we're dealing with something that might be paranormal?"

"All right. Fine. *If* we are dealing with something... paranormal, then we need to go see someone."

16

Madame Ethelinda was helping a customer when Mason and Bill walked into her shop. The man at the counter had a handful of crystals and wanted her to tell him which one to buy so that he would get a promotion at work and make his ex-wife jealous enough to take him back. Madame Ethelinda was trying to explain to him that crystals did not work like that.

"Bullshit," the man said. He pounded his fist on the counter. "My wife...ex-wife... told me *all* about this little store and these magic rocks that can do whatever you want them to. Just tell me which one will do it."

"Okay. All right," Madame Ethelinda replied, exaggerating her already thick accent. She looked over at Mason and Bill and gave them a knowing wink despite not actually knowing that they were coming. "For what you desire you will need these four." She bagged up the crystals for the man as he swiped his credit card.

The man took the bag from the counter and before pushing his way through Mason and Bill on his way out of the shop. Once the door had closed, Madame Ethelinda came around the counter to greet them.

"Those crystals won't do what he wants," Bill said.

"You are right," Madame Ethelinda said, "but they *did* do exactly what I wanted."

Bill laughed.

"Some people believe. Others do not. Some of those who don't can open their minds over time and see the truth. He is not one who ever will. How are you Mason? I must say, I am surprised you are here without Amber."

"I probably wouldn't be if I had a choice." He looked down and wrung his hands. "We need your help. Amber is missing."

"Ah." Madame Ethelinda led them to the table at the back of the store. The three of them kicked off their shoes and knelt at the table. Madame Ethelinda lit the candle just like she had before.

She opened a drawer and took out a small velvet bag.

"Did you bring anything of hers?"

Mason handed her Amber's cell phone.

"Good," she said. She opened the map app and had Mason enter the address where he last saw Amber.

Madame Ethelinda chanted something in a language that neither Mason nor Bill recognized. She began pulling oils and powders out of the bag and sprinkled them on the phone. Her eyes rolled into the back of her head.

Ruby and Timmy, who were watching over her shoulder as she worked, began vibrating.

Wind chimes throughout the shop started ringing. A cold breeze swirled around the table. Then it was hot. Bill's glasses clouded with steam. Ruby and Timmy began vibrating faster and looked like they were beginning to dissolve.

Mason held his breath for what felt like an hour. In reality, the entire ritual was finished in about thirty seconds. The air stopped swirling, the chimes stopped ringing, Ruby and Timmy reappeared. Madame Ethelinda slid the phone across the table and blew out the candle.

Mason looked at the phone. There was a pin on the map.

"That is where you will find Amber."

Mason leapt to his feet and grabbed his shoes. He was halfway to the door before Madame Ethelinda stopped him.

"Before you go, there's something you must know," she said.

She walked over to the cash register.

"Can't I pay you later?" Mason said. "Amber could be in serious danger."

"She is. That is why you must see this." She bent down below the counter and grabbed a book. It had a thick leather cover with a gold buckle holding it closed. Madame Ethelinda blew a layer of dust off of the buckle and opened the book.

After flipping through the pages, Madame Ethelinda dropped the book on the counter. A plume of dust flew up from the pages. Bill adjusted his glasses and looked down. Mason's mouth fell open when he saw the hand-drawn sketch in the book.

"What's this," Bill asked. Mason already knew. Wiry hair, gray skin, sunken eyes, and sharp, discolored teeth. The only things missing were the lobotomy holes and it could have been a picture of Eliza.

"*This* is who took Amber," Madame Ethelinda said. "You must be careful. Very little is known of these creatures. Most who have met them did not live to tell about it.

"Many cultures have stories of a lost tribe or dark tricksters. The legend of these creatures is much the same. As the others began to settle, they remained nomads. But their food became scarce and they were forced into cannibalism.

"The legend says that when the animals were gone, they ate the women of the tribe first. They put up less of a fight and their meat was much more tender than the men. At night, they would sneak into villages and stab the sleeping men with sharpened sticks. Their laughter filled the village with a sense of dread.

"To them, torture was a game and by scaring other tribes into not leaving their villages, they were able to keep themselves hidden. But over time, they had to change. Once all of the women in the tribe were gone, they needed more food and a way to keep their tribe from dying out.

"It is said that was when they developed their abilities. Some say they are able to paralyze a man with nothing more than a look. Others believe that they have the power to hypnotize. They use laughter to confuse and disorient their victims. If it is loud, they are far away and the closer they are the quieter it sounds."

"That's a hell of a story," Mason said dismissively but his entire body was covered in a cold layer of sweat.

"Do these things have a name?" Bill asked.

"They do. But I will not say it. Legend says that anyone who speaks their name will not live through another night."

"Anything else?" Mason said. He looked at the map on Amber's phone and began tapping his foot.

"No. Go. But know what you are getting yourselves into," she said. She slid the book into Bill's hands. "Take this. And be careful."

Bill locked eyes with Madame Ethelinda for a moment. He picked up the book and nodded. He left a business card on the counter in its place.

"I would love to talk to you for my podcast when things don't feel quite so... *murdery*," he said as he followed Mason out the door.

60 YEARS AGO

"Don't go far, Eliza. Dinner will be ready soon."

"Okay Mom," Eliza called from halfway across the yard. The sun was just starting to drop over the horizon. Eliza was wearing her pinstripe windbreaker and Yankees cap. She flipped her hat around so the bill followed her ponytail down her back. She was heading toward the trees. At the start of the summer, her mom had helped her build a pitching mound so she could practice her curveball.

Eliza stepped onto the mound and kicked the rubber with her sneaker. She shook off a couple of imaginary signs before getting the one she wanted.

Once she had the sign, she spat toward first base and looked back at the pretend runner on second before throwing the pitch. The red ball bounced off Eliza's plywood catcher into the trees.

Eliza punched her hand into her glove and dropped it as she chased after her ball. Each time she thought she had caught up to the ball, it took a weird bounce and stayed just out of her reach. It bounced around trees and off rocks like it had a mind of its own. As she chased it farther into the forest, her imaginary crowd of cheering fans started to laugh.

The sun continued to drop and the sky grew darker. The laughing crowd was loud at first but as she chased the ball deeper into the woods, it grew quiet. She almost had it. The ball ricocheted off of a rock and out of the trees onto the highway. Eliza did not hesitate. She knew she was supposed to stay away from the road when she was alone—even when someone was with her, she was supposed to stop and look before crossing—but the ball was right there. And no one ever drove down this highway. She lunged onto the asphalt. Her fingers closed around the ball and she stood up, ball in hand, smiling with pride.

And then she saw the headlights.

Her eyes got wide. The ball fell out of her hand. It bounced. The tires on the truck began to squeal. Eliza squeezed her eyes shut as hard as she could. Her crowd started laughing again. Eliza clenched her entire body and waited for the collision.

Something hit her shoulder, but it was not the truck. And then her feet were off of the ground.

Eliza opened her eyes. She was looking straight up into the purple sky through the treetops. The first stars of the night were beginning to shine.

She was being carried by two things. They looked almost like people. *Almost*. Their bodies were barely more than tanned gray skin stretched over a Halloween-store skeleton. The one carrying her by her shoulders was smiling. The bottoms of all its teeth were sharpened to a point.

Eliza wanted to scream. She couldn't. Nothing came out. The thing carrying her shoulders seemed to hear her anyway. It looked down at her. Its eyes had no white in them, just two pools of pure black. She saw her reflection in them.

And then she did not want to scream anymore. She wanted to laugh.

And she did.

17

Mason drove when they left Madame Ethelinda's shop. Bill wanted to be able to look closer at the book.

"Wow, look at this. There's an entire section in here about a town in North Dakota," Bill said. "It's called Paradise. From the look of this, it's anything but."

"Would you focus? You can geek out later. Right now we need a plan."

"Right. Right." Bill flipped back to the page that Madame Ethelinda had shown them. "There's not really much here that she didn't already tell us."

"Keep looking." Mason stopped at a red light. He drummed on the steering wheel and his right foot hovered over the gas pedal, waiting for the light to turn green.

"Here's something. It says they can paralyze and hypnotize people just by looking at them. And they will use sound tricks to disorient and confuse us."

"So we can't look at them or listen to them. How exactly is that supposed to help?"

"If they can't trick us or hypnotize us, we will be able to fight back."

"How can we fight something without seeing or hearing it?"

"Just stop off at your house and get your bike. I have something that should be able to help us. We'll meet back at the forest in an hour."

Mason drove to his house and got out of the car.

"Whatever you're getting better work. We shouldn't be wasting time."

"It will. One hour. We won't be able to save her without it."

***

Mason paced back and forth in the kitchen, checking his watch each time he reached the other end of the room.

"T-take it e-easy, would you? You're g-going to wear a h-hole in the floor," Timmy said.

"Take it easy? You want me to take it easy when I know that Amber is out there being tortured and I have to just wait around doing nothing?"

"No. He's right, love," Ruby said. "Marching around like that'll do nobody any good."

"I don't care! They killed my dog while he was sleeping on top of me for God's sake. And now they have Amber."

"What are you going to do about it then?" she asked.

"I don't know! That's the problem. Bill has an idea but I don't know what it is. That book makes those things—who by the way look exactly like Eliza—seem invincible. Why is that anyway? She was just a normal girl right? Why does she look like that?"

Eliza was in the dining room, staring out the window and hugging her ball to her chest.

"Didn't that old l-lady say they a-ate all of their w-women?"

"Yeah, so?"

"S-so th-they couldn't h-have children without w-women, right? Maybe that's why they kidnapped her."

"Brilliant. They can't make their own kids so they steal somebody else's," Ruby said.

"But why does she look like them?"

"M-maybe that's part of the hypnosis or s-something. They can literally t-t-turn those kids into their own."

"That's great. So if they don't eat Amber, they will turn her into one of them. And we have no idea how to stop them."

"No. We don't," said Ruby. "But someone does." She nodded toward Eliza.

"Th-that's right. They had h-her for two weeks trying to t-turn her and she found a way to escape."

"Okay genius. You figure out how she did it. She can't talk, remember?" Mason looked at his watch again. "I don't have time for this." He grabbed the keys and his helmet off of the arm of the couch on his way out the door.

Ruby and Timmy chased him across the yard.

"Why can't you take the car?" Ruby called out as Mason pulled the helmet down onto his head. "Like it or not we are tethered to you. It would be nice to at least have a place to sit."

Mason raised his visor and swung a leg over the seat of his Valkyrie.

"Not my problem," he said. He flipped the visor closed and took off.

60 YEARS AGO

Eliza's new family had not said a single word. None of them even knew how to speak. But they laughed.

They all laughed, all of the time. Life was beautiful. It was easy to find the joy and humor in even the smallest things, like stabbing a squirrel—or a dog—with a spear that she had sharpened with her own teeth.

Eliza had a home with a family that loved her as she was. One that encouraged her to be what she wanted to be, to eat what she wanted to eat, kill what she wanted to kill, and enjoy every minute of it.

She was happy. Eliza did not even remember life before her new family found her. All she remembered was that she never felt good enough.

Eliza had been with them for a week and she had not even once thought about baseball.

18

Mason pulled off the highway near where they had crossed before Amber had been taken. He looked at his watch. The hour Bill had asked for was almost up, but there was no sign of his Escalade. Mason's forearms grew itchy. He took to walking the length of his motorcycle.

"Now that is a good place to pace," Ruby said. "The road is paved and if you do manage to wear it out you won't have to worry about replacing it yourself."

Timmy tried to laugh but threw himself into an asthma attack instead. Mason's eyes narrowed to slits and he stopped walking.

"Sorry love, just trying to lighten the mood."

"You get anything out of Eliza?"

"Not a peep," Ruby said.

"I don't th-think she remembers any of it. Could b-be what she n-needs you for."

"If she forgot about it, why would she want to remember?"

"L-look at her. I don't think sh-she knows who—or wh-what—she is. If you were a kid and couldn't remember who you were, wouldn't you want to know?"

"Could explain that weird flashing bit," Ruby said.

"So what? Being around them was helping her remember?"

"I think so," Timmy said.

Eliza was standing in the middle of the highway, staring straight down at the road. She squatted and set her ball on the pavement. With one hand, she rubbed the road. Her other hand went up to her temple. As she ran her fingers along the side of her head, she changed. It lasted longer than before. The holes on the sides of her vanished. Her greasy hair became a red pony tail hanging down from under a Yankees ball cap. Her gray skin flushed with color. She had clusters of freckles on both of her cheeks. She looked at Mason. The blackness in her eyes lightened into a bright kelly green.

A black SUV came around a curve in the road a half-mile behind Eliza. She heard the car and turned toward the sound. The distraction interrupted whatever was happening to her and she reverted to her usual, horrifying appearance. Eliza hissed in the direction of Bill's car, grabbed her ball, and ran to the shoulder. She hunkered down at the base of a tree. Mason held his arm up and tapped the face of his watch as Bill stepped onto the road with a box in his hands.

"You're late."

"I'm here now. Are you ready?" Bill said.

Bill set the box down between them and opened it. He pulled out two sets of goggles and two pairs of noise-cancelling headphones.

"You needed an hour for this?"

"I had to make a few adjustments. I normally use these for ghost hunting, not sensory deprivation."

Bill put on one of the pairs of goggles and saw Eliza crouched under a tree on the side of the road. He jumped backward and tripped over the box, ripping the goggles off as he fell to the ground.

"It's here. One of those things. It's watching us."

He pointed a shaky finger at Eliza. Ruby and Timmy laughed. So did Mason.

"No. That's just Eliza. But hey, at least your ghost glasses work." He reached out a hand to help Bill to his feet. Bill brushed the loose gravel from his pants and put his goggles back on. Mason did the same.

"When I start the program, it will overlay the map from Amber's phone on the lenses. That way we won't actually be looking at what we are seeing, just a live stream of what's in front of us."

"And these?" Mason held up the headphones.

"We don't know how their powers work so we have to cover all the bases. If we don't look at them and can't hear them, then they should not be able to hypnotize us."

"Okay. But how do we stop them if we find them? They will still try to kill us."

"We kill them first," Bill said matter-of-factly. He walked back to his Escalade and opened the back door. On the seat were two hunting rifles. They each took a gun and Bill pushed a button on his phone. A blue line appeared in the lenses of the goggles with an arrow leading them into the trees. There was a number at the bottom of Mason's vision. *4.29.*

"That's how far away Amber is. Just follow the line. And keep your eyes open. The goggles have motion sensors so that should let us know if any of them get close. Good luck."

With that, they put on their headphones and headed off into the forest.

***

It felt strange walking through the forest, unable to hear anything except for his own heartbeat inside his skull. Mason tried not to think about what they might be walking toward as he followed the blue arrow floating in front of him.

Bill kept his shoulder pressed against Mason's as they walked. Every few steps, he spun along Mason's back to the other side, checking behind them to make sure they were not being followed. The number at the bottom of the goggles counted down.

3.5.

2.7.

1.3.

Ruby and Timmy carried Eliza between them. Ruby said something, but because of the headphones, Mason did not know what. That was a relief. Part of him still wanted to believe that this was all in his head, that it was not really happening. But if it was in his head, the headphones probably wouldn't work.

A red light pulsed in a tree ahead of them. Bill tapped Mason's shoulder and pointed. Mason nodded. They both raised their rifles. The blinking light moved down the trunk of the tree and darted across the trail in front of him. *Just a squirrel.*

Mason exhaled heavily. They had been walking for forty-five minutes when they came to a pile of downed tree trunks blocking the path. Amber had to be just on the other side. The distance on their goggles was down to ***0.01***.

There had been no sign of movement since the squirrel. Mason was starting to believe their plan might actually work.

Ruby and Timmy had resorted to dragging Eliza. Her legs stopped moving just over a mile back.

Bill kept up his best SWAT impression, checking their surroundings with the scope on his rifle. He was about to pull another spin move along Mason's back. Mason grabbed the barrel of Bill's rifle to stop him. He mimed climbing over the logs. Bill nodded. Mason had both hands and a foot on the rotting tree trunks when he saw Ruby jumping and waving her arms above her head. Timmy was struggling to keep Eliza on her feet by himself. Mason grabbed Bill's arm to keep him from climbing.

Ruby gestured for them to come toward her. Mason turned to motion for Bill to follow him, but Bill was a step ahead of him. More proof that he was not crazy. Bill could see Ruby.

Ruby led them off the trail. Behind a small cluster of trees, the log wall ended. They could just walk around it.

Ruby left them to go help Timmy with Eliza before he ended up dying again. Mason and Bill turned around the logs. It was getting late and everything was silhouetted by the angle of the sun.

Hanging by a rope from a low branch on one of the trees was a dark shape. Mason started to run toward it but Bill grabbed his shirt to slow him down. Bill tapped the side of his forehead when Mason looked at him. *Be smart.* They did not know for sure that it was Amber hanging from the tree. And even if it was her, they had no way to know who—*or what*—else might be waiting for them.

They stayed near the wall as they crept toward the silhouette. Bill resumed scanning their sides and behind them. Mason focused only on Amber. It *had* to be her.

As they got closer, the sun continued to drop. The scene came into focus. The log wall crossed the trail just before a clearing in the forest. There were only a couple of trees in the clearing. Hanging from one of the trees was a blonde woman in a denim jacket, with dirt and blood caked in her hair. The rope was wrapped under her arms and between her legs. Her head hung limply, hair draped over her face. But Mason had known Amber since they were nine years old. It was her.

Mason took one quick look around the clearing. There was no one and nothing in sight. He lowered the rifle and ran to her. Bill reached out to grab him, but did not catch him in time. So instead, he stayed five steps behind with his rifle up, trying to keep Mason covered in case anything came at him.

Mason reached Amber and turned her in her harness. He dropped the rifle and put his hands on her cheeks. Her breathing was shallow. Streaks of blood were drying on the sides of her head. He tilted her head up and rested her forehead against his own. Her eyes were half-open. His eyes drifted down. The left leg of her pants was ripped. All that remained of her hamstring were a few strands of muscle and the bone.

"Oh God. Amber. What did they do to you?"

She let out a soft moan. He moved his hands from her face to her shoulders and rubbed them. Her jacket was soaked with blood. He opened it and pulled her left arm out of the sleeve. Her shoulder looked just like her thigh. Most of it was gone. The edges were not cut cleanly, it looked like an animal ripped the meat from her bones with its teeth.

There was another wet spot at the bottom of her jacket, near her right hip. Mason was afraid to look. He knew he would find more of the same.

Mason brought his head up to Amber's and kissed her forehead.

"I'm going to get you out of here."

He began working on untying the rope. His cousin had been an Eagle Scout so he had seen some strong knots before, but never one like this. He patted his pockets. While he had been pacing in their kitchen waiting for Bill, he had grabbed his pocket knife out of the drawer. He found it and flipped open the two-inch blade. Mason pulled the rope away from the back of Amber's neck and began sawing at it. Slowly, the strands began to fray.

Bill held his position several steps away from them, watching for any signs of movement. Mason kept cutting.

As the last strand of rope snapped and Amber dropped into Mason's arms, she finally realized what was happening. She wrapped her one good arm around him and buried her face in the crook of his neck.

She started thanking him and crying but Mason could not hear her. He was still wearing the headphones. Once Amber was cut loose, Bill took one more sweeping glance around the clearing before going to help keep Amber on her feet. He ducked under her injured arm and lifted his neck into her armpit, holding her up so she could use him like a crutch.

"You're going to be okay," Bill said.

Mason leaned his head against hers. Amber was turned to the side away from Bill. She screamed.

Mason felt something pierce his side, just below his rib cage. He pushed Bill and Amber away and fell to his knees. A three-foot long tree branch was sticking out of his side.

"Get out of here," he yelled at Amber. She was trying to break away from Bill to run to Mason. She managed to get away from Bill, but the missing muscle in her leg made it impossible to stand on her own and she collapsed. Bill helped her back to her feet and pulled her away from Mason. Amber was still screaming.

Mason stared at Bill.

"Take her home," he said, slowly to make sure Bill could read his lips. "No matter what happens, don't come back. You make sure she is safe."

Bill nodded and pulled Amber away. Mason ripped the branch

out of his side, tossed the headphones off of his ears, and stretched out on the ground for his rifle.

He used the butt of the rifle to push himself to his feet. It did not look like there was anything in the clearing with him, but there was laughter and whistling coming from all directions. Red dots blinked all over his field of vision. There was something—or lots of things—darting around the edges of the clearing. Mason could not see anything behind the red dots. He aimed at one and fired. Then another and another. And two more. He tried to keep shooting but instead of firing when he pulled the trigger, the gun clicked. *Out of ammo.*

He flipped the gun around and held it by the barrel. He held the butt of the rifle up behind his ear and raised his elbow up just like his little league coach had taught him. He was going to die—of that he was sure—but he would do his best to take some of them out with him.

He did not get the chance.

Another tree-branch spear hit him just above the knee and he felt a blow on the back of his head.

60 YEARS AGO

After a long night of hunting baby animals in the forest, Eliza climbed up into a tree near the clearing to get some rest. The sun was beginning to rise.

They were not supposed to go near the road to hunt. In fact, they were not even supposed to go near any other clearings. Stay in the woods. That was the only rule.

But Eliza *had* gone to the road. She followed a baby deer that was separated from its mother. It ignored her laughing and did not seem confused at all.

Eliza wanted to catch it. She had not seen any other animals all night and she was hungry, so she followed it right up to the edge of the highway. After three tries with her spear, she managed to hit it, just before it crossed the road. Her aim was getting better.

Eliza's teeth had not fully sharpened. It took her the rest of the night to rip the meat off of the deer's bones, but she stayed until she had eaten every scrap.

She let out a loud laugh when she finished—a celebratory cheer of sorts. It was her first night hunting alone and she had eaten well.

As she stood up from the shoulder of the highway—belly full, face covered in blood, smiling ear-to-ear—something caught her eye. It looked like a fuzzy rock. She picked it up. It was much lighter than a rock.

Eliza carried it with her back to the clearing. She climbed into her tree and held it up in the moonlight. Whatever it was, she liked the way it felt in her hands. And it was the same color as the blood on her face. Her favorite color. *Red.*

Eliza did not sleep. She rolled the ball in her hands. It felt familiar. It felt *right.* The more she looked at the ball, the more she wondered about her life before waking up in the clearing two weeks ago.

The sun brought memories with it as it continued to rise. Her name was Eliza. She lived with her parents in a house on the other side of the highway. She wanted to be a baseball player. She did not belong in the woods.

She jumped down from her tree and started walking. From the trees around the clearing, she heard the others start whistling. They usually laughed. They only whistled when they were angry.

Eliza did not care. She wanted to go home. She held the ball to her chest as she walked. The whistling grew louder. Once she left the clearing, it stopped.

She heard branches rustling over her head as the others raced past her. She kept walking. Two screams rang out from the other side of the highway. Still she kept walking.

Eliza crossed the highway. When she entered the trees on the other side, she saw the others. They hissed and snarled as she approached them. Eliza did not slow down.

When the others realized that she was not going to stop, they jumped back into the trees. Eliza kept walking until her foot hit something on the trail. She stopped for a moment to look down. Two bodies were lying on the ground. *Dead*. Like the ball, the bodies seemed familiar, but she did not recognize them.

When she came to the edge of the forest, she walked parallel to the trees until she found the driveway. She was home.

19

The blow to the head had knocked Mason unconscious. When he came to, he did not know how long he had been out, but it was dark. He was tied up in the same tree that he had cut Amber down from.

Everything hurt. He tried to get his hands or feet free but the knots holding him were just as strong as they had been when he found Amber.

"I t-told you he wasn't dead."

Ruby and Timmy were sitting on the ground below him with their cribbage board. A full moon illuminated the clearing. Eliza was sitting on a branch in the tree next to the one Mason was hanging from. Mason looked around the clearing. They appeared to be alone.

"Can you guys get me down from here?"

Ruby laid her cards on the ground and stood up.

"Be happy to love, but—what with being a ghost and all—can't."

"Right. What did I miss?"

"They t-tied you up and took turns st-stabbing you."

"That part I had pretty much worked out on my own, thanks." Mason's harness rotated. He winced. "Anything else?"

"Not really, no," Ruby said. "The sun went down and they all left."

That was good. It meant he had time to come up with a way out of this.

"What about her?" Mason nodded toward the tree behind him.

"Not a clue."

"She cl-climbed up there as soon as we got h-here."

Eliza was changing again. Each time Mason spun so that he was able to see her tree, she looked different. First she was one of those monsters. Then a normal little girl.

Maybe she was remembering.

They did not say anything else for the next hour. Every few minutes a laugh drifted into the clearing with the cold breeze. Mason was still wearing the goggles. He had given up trying to wriggle out of the rope and his eyes were beginning to close when a flashing red dot appeared in front of him.

"They're coming back," Mason whispered. "Can they see you? Do you need to hide?"

"No. I think they can s-sense s-something, but they can't see us."

"Not unless we want them to," Ruby said.

Five creatures arrived in the clearing, each with shoulder-length or longer hair, hollow cheeks, and a mouthful of daggers. Four of them sat down in front of Mason. The fifth jumped up into the tree above him and broke off five small branches.

They sat in a row, all staring at Mason. Mason stared back. Then, they all laughed and began dragging the tips of the sticks across their teeth. They were whittling spears—spears to stab him with, probably to kill him with—and they were making him watch.

"Sure there's nothing you can do to get me out of here?" Mason said.

"Sorry, love."

"How about dealing me in for the next game then?"

Ruby laughed. Mason looked up at the things—they all looked like they could be children in Halloween costumes—sharpening murder weapons in front of him. He took a deep breath and put on his used car smile.

"Hey fellas," he said. "Nice night isn't it?"

No response.

"Looks like you live out here. What do you say we make a deal? I can hook you guys up with some top-of-the-line tree houses. Just use those nice sharp sticks you've got there and cut me down. We'll work out the other details later."

One of his captors stood up. It walked toward Mason, taking the stick out of its mouth and placing it in one of its hands. It reached the other hand toward the rope.

Its hand stopped short of the rope and covered Mason's face. Fingernails—almost as sharp as its teeth—dug into Mason's forehead and cheeks. Then it started to spin him.

Its other hand brought the stick up and stabbed Mason in the shoulder. Then the stomach. Then the back of his leg. Then the chest. Each thrust deeper than the last. All five creatures roared with laughter. One of the others fell over and rolled around on the ground.

The others got up to join in on the fun. Mason remembered something from Madame Ethelinda's book. They liked to torture people before they killed them. Something to do with the hormones making the meat more flavorful. *Maybe*. Did they just kill men or did they eat them too? Mason could not remember. He supposed it would not matter what they did once he was dead. They could do whatever they wanted with his body as long as he was not alive to feel it.

They had all lined up, waiting for their turn to play with Mason. Just as the second one stepped toward him, Mason heard a voice call out.

"Stop!" It was a voice Mason had never heard before. A child's voice.

Eliza dropped out of the tree. And it *was* Eliza. The real Eliza—a redheaded, freckle-faced, Yankees fan. She walked toward them until she was standing between Mason and his attackers. As she walked, a purple light seemed to shine out of her, growing brighter with each step.

"Do you remember me?" Eliza said to the creatures. They growled in response. "I remember you. I remember everything."

Eliza tossed her ball straight up and waited for it to fall back into her hand.

"I know you all like to have fun. But killing people isn't fun. It's bad. I know a game that is way more fun."

Mason's captors looked at each other with furrowed brows. Then back at Eliza.

"It's called baseball. I could stay and teach you, you know. But only if you let my friend go. And no more kidnapping or killing people."

"What are you doing?" Mason said. "You can't stay with these things. You just got back to normal. You can talk again. I can't let you trade yourself for me."

"You can't stop me," Eliza said to Mason. "Thanks to you, I know who I am again. I remember everything that happened to me. I owe you for that. Besides, I miss baseball."

Eliza smiled at Mason. One of her front teeth had fallen out before she died and the other had only halfway grown in.

She turned back toward the creatures.

"So... what do you say? Do you want to play with me?"

They looked at each other again. One of them seemed to nod. The leader—or at least the one Mason thought of as the leader—walked past Eliza and pointed the stick at Mason's face. Then it spun him around and cut the rope. Mason fell to the ground.

"I can't just leave you here," Mason said to the little girl standing in front of him.

"Yes you can. And you will. I want to stay anyway. I started working on my curveball sixty years ago and I've been dying to try it out."

Mason staggered to his feet and ran out of the clearing. He looked back over his shoulder after a couple of steps.

"Thank you, Mason," she called after him. "I don't know how I could ever repay you."

"I think you just did. And then some."

20

The sun was up by the time Mason got back to his motorcycle. Ruby and Timmy were by his side, but no one said so much as a word. That changed as soon as Mason threw his leg over the bike.

"Here we go again. You know every time you ride that thing, it's like you're pulling us by a rope tied around our waists?" Ruby said.

Mason looked at his phone. There was a text message from Bill.

At hospital. Amber ok. If you make it out of this, got a job for you.

"Last time. I promise," said Mason. He left his helmet on the shoulder of the highway as he took off, letting the wind blow through his hair.

As he rode along Highway 63, he thought about what Amber had said right before she was taken.

"You need to be able to decide what it is that you want."

He had almost lost her. Then, he found her and almost lost her again. He didn't need to decide. He knew. No matter what else happened, he wanted to be with her. For the rest of his life.

Mason turned off of the highway into the parking lot at *Uncle Jim's.*

"Didn't expect to see you back yet," Jim said as he came over to shake Mason's hand. "Whoa. What happened to you?" Mason's clothes were full of holes covered in dried blood.

"You wouldn't believe me if I told you," Mason said.

"Try me."

"Maybe another time."

"Okay. But I can't let you work looking like that."

"I'm not here to work," Mason said. "Actually, I was hoping to take that VW bus off of your hands. If you've still got it."

Jim called Jeremy to bring the van from the back lot. Mason never had gotten around to doing all of the work on it so Jim had to keep it hidden.

While they waited for Jeremy to bring the van around, Jim put away his salesman persona.

"Haven't heard from Amber in a while. I know you kids were working through something. Everything all right?"

"It will be," Mason said. And he actually believed it.

Jeremy pulled up with the van and handed Mason the keys.

"I thought you were never getting rid of your bike," he said. "What? Are you starting a family or something?"

"Yeah," Mason turned to look at Ruby and Timmy, "something like that."

"Looks like you had a rough night," Jim said. "Why don't you just leave the Valkyrie and swing by later this week. We'll take care of the paperwork then and you can tell me when you'll be coming back to work."

"Thanks Jim. But... I don't think I will be coming back. Going to take a shot with a new opportunity that came up."

Jim nodded to him and headed toward his office with Jeremy.

"Lookit that," Ruby said, "something with seats."

Mason spun the key ring around his finger.

"Yeah. I thought it was appropriate. Since it looks like we're going to keep doing this sort of thing, I thought we might need a van. Like *Scooby-Doo.*"

"Who's Scooby?"

"A-and wh-what did he d-do?"

Mason chuckled.

"Just get in. We've got one more stop to make on the way to the hospital."

WANT MORE?

VISIT WWW.SHAWNWINCHELL.COM/JOIN

FOR AN EXCLUSIVE EPISODE OF BILL'S PODCAST

I hope that you enjoyed reading this book as much as I enjoyed writing it. If you did, please consider leaving a review on Amazon.

I could tell everyone myself that they will enjoy reading my book, but it means more coming from another reader who has already enjoyed the book.

Word of mouth is the best way for you to help an author be able to write the next book.

I would love to hear what you thought of it.

Reach out and let me know at:

www.shawnwinchell.com

or

www.facebook.com/authorshawnwinchell

Made in the USA
Coppell, TX
17 July 2021

59083716R00132